HORSE of TWO COLORS

HORSE
OF TWO
COLORS

BY GLENN BALCH

Illustrated by Lorence Bjorklund

THOMAS Y. CROWELL COMPANY   NEW YORK

To Holly Kalani Cummings

BY THE AUTHOR

The Brave Riders
The Flaxy Mare
Horse in Danger
Horse of Two Colors
Keeping Horse
The Stallion King
Stallion's Foe
Tiger Roan

HORSE of TWO COLORS

CHAPTER 1

The earthen blocks that formed the high, strong Spanish wall moved and loosened. Gradually a small opening appeared, which soon became a big, dark, ragged hole. Out of this blackness then came a slim figure, leading what seemed, in the vague starlight, to be a white horse. Clearing the hole, the youth turned and whispered behind him, "Come on, Pansook! Hurry!"

A second figure emerged from the hole, also leading a horse. This horse, in the dimness of the night, was hardly more than a shadowy movement. Pansook at first had not intended to take a horse and had gone back for one only when he discovered how easy it would be.

"Hurry!" the first youth repeated urgently, in the guttural language of the Eutaw Indian tribe. "We must get away from here quickly. I fear that some of the bearded men may have heard the noise."

The "bearded men" were the Spaniards. The thick,

dark hair that grew on their faces was a strange sight to these young Indians, who had never seen any other white men.

It was the year 1680, and the walled stockade stood in what is now the state of New Mexico. The settlement was the northernmost of the thin chain of Spanish villages extending upward from the great blue curve of the Gulf of Mexico, out of which the sturdy ships of the conquistadores had first appeared. Here, in this empty land, they had built houses and had surrounded them with the high, strong walls for protection against the dangers of that wild and un-known country.

The first boy, Mots-kay, wheeled and ran into the night, as swiftly as the large white shape at his heels would follow. Pan-sook ran too, with a long, easy stride that was quickly matched by the horse he led. Though they had seen the Spaniards ride horses, the two youths were not yet sure it could be done by Indians.

"It has been a long time," Pan-sook sang out softly but joyously. "I am happy to be out of that place. There were times when I was afraid we would never escape."

There had been times when Mots-kay, too, had thought that, times when everything had seemed completely hopeless. But now he was supremely happy. After two long years of captivity he and Pan-sook were finally free, and he was started on the long journey back to the land of his people, the Nimapus.

Much had happened to Mots-kay in those two years. First there had been a long journey southward, so that he and the men of the Nimapu tribe could trade with the Shoshonee Indians for horses. Then, before they had started back home, their new horses —and most of the Shoshonee horses as well—had been stolen in a daring night raid by a band of Eutaw Indians. In the pursuit of the Eutaws that followed, Mots-kay and his new Shoshonee friend, Pan-sook, had been captured. The two boys had been kept as slaves for long months in a Eutaw village. There they had been humiliated by having to do hated "woman's work." However, of necessity they had learned the Eutaw language, which they now used, since neither could speak the other's native tongue.

Some months later, on a visit to the Spanish settlement, the Eutaws traded the two young slaves for horses. Mots-kay and Pan-sook then spent many more long months as *cristianos*—the name the Spaniards gave to their Indian workers.

Cristiano meant "convert to Christianity" for the Spaniards never called their Indians "slaves." But the only difference Mots-kay and Pan-sook noticed between their existence in the Eutaw village and their life among the Spaniards was in the type of work they were required to do. In the Spanish settlement they were put to work in the horse pens, scooping the manure into big baskets. This was better than carrying wood and scraping hides under the fault-finding eyes of the Eutaw women. However, the chains on their ankles and the bar across the door of their small hut at night made it amply plain that their status as prisoners had not changed.

The Spaniards had many *cristianos*. The others were Indians from the surrounding tribes, who were made to work in the fields outsice the high wall. But the huts they slept in were usually unlocked, and, except to see that they had plenty of work to do, the Spaniards paid little attention to them. None of the local *cristianos* were permitted to handle the horses.

The truth was that the Spaniards did not want their Indians to know about horses—to realize how gentle and useful the big creatures could be or what a great boon it was to be carried on their backs. This knowledge, the white men were afraid, would result in danger to themselves and their settlement. But, there was much work to be done at the horse pens, and it was tedious and tiring—and the two new young Indians were from distant and unknown tribes. They could not even speak the same language as the other *cristianos*. Surely, the Spaniards thought, no harm could come from letting the two boys do the monotonous work of cleaning the pens and car-

4

rying the manure baskets to the fields. They were plainly too shy and frightened to try anything harmful.

Mots-kay and Pan-sook *were* shy and frightened, at first. They became good *cristianos,* willing and obedient, doing as they were told—but, secretly, their sharp eyes missed nothing that went on about them. The Spaniards were fooled. Not many weeks passed before they began to relax their precautions. First the chains were taken from the ankles of the two youths, and a few nights later no one came to put the heavy bar across the hut door.

"Come!" Pan-sook whispered jubilantly that night. "Now we can escape. We can climb to the top of one of the sheds and jump over the wall. No one will see us."

Mots-kay considered this seriously. He was anxious to escape too. But he said, "The distance to our homes is too great. The way is rough and hazardous, and we have nothing—no bows and arrows, nor robes and moccasins. There will be much danger and hardship. It is best that we wait until we can get the things that we will need so badly on the long journey." Pan-sook had to agree—though reluctantly. A gnawing impatience to get back to his village was growing inside him.

Among the things Mots-kay thought they needed for their journey were the Spaniards' long knives.

Though his people practically depended for their lives on the use of cutting edges, Mots-kay had never imagined that knives of such hard, thin material existed. Why, with a knife like that, so strong and quickly sharpened, there was little that a man could not do, he thought.

In the matter of acquiring a knife, Mots-kay had luck. He found one while he was scything grass for the penned horses in a field nearby. Bright and sharp and hardly used, the knife had doubtless been lost by some galloping Spaniard. Now it was carefully hidden inside Mots-kay's baggy *cristiano* shirt. The Indian youth also carried there a small bundle of meat, to which he had stealthily added, night after night, from the pan in which he was given his food.

Pan-sook had a similar bundle of meat, and a fine knife too, though at first Mots-kay had dared hope for only one. Pan-sook had taken his knife from a table in one of the houses, when the woman who fixed their food pans was not looking. Pan-sook had cool courage when it was needed.

They did not have much—hardly more meat than they could have eaten in one meal, and two strong, long-bladed knives—but to the young Indians it was enough to give them the hope and confidence necessary for the great journey.

"Your people will be happy when they see you come home leading a fine horse," Mots-kay said.

"Yes," Pan-sook agreed joyfully. "Many moons have passed since the day we set out in pursuit of the horse thieves. And much," he added, his mood changing rapidly, "has happened."

Mots-kay knew how his companion felt, for the months had been long and depressing. He said, "It is all right now. Now we are started for our homes."

Pan-sook did not answer. But before Mots-kay could say any more, an outcry rose into the night air from behind the wall of the Spanish compound. It was filled with anger and alarm, and was followed an instant later by a booming sound.

"They know that we have escaped," Pan-sook muttered as they ran.

"Yes, but perhaps they do not know yet that we have taken two of their fine horses," Mots-kay replied hopefully.

Both of them knew well that the stealing of a horse by an Indian, and especially by one of the *cristianos,* was considered by the Spaniards to be an unforgivable crime. Harsh and immediate punishment was given to all such offenders if they were caught.

Pan-sook quickened his stride and answered, "We must go as swiftly as we can, for they will soon know it. They will come searching for us in the dark."

The booming had been the sound of a gun, or "smoke-stick," which to Mots-kay was one of the most fearsome and bewildering things in all the astounding magic apparatus possessed by the Spaniards. The great booming noise and the cloud of black smoke that belched from the end of the smokestick were hard to understand. No wonder these bearded men had been able to come safely on the great journey from their homes in a far-off country.

The two youths were hurrying steadily through the darkness when the horse Mots-kay was leading suddenly pulled back and lifted his big angular head. Then the quietness was shattered by a loud, resounding neigh.

Mots-kay, with his habits of stealth and silence, was so shocked and dismayed that he could hardly speak. "No, no!" he managed to say. "Be quiet, Spotted One!" How could such a splendid horse be so noisy and stupid?

Pan-sook was equally shocked. "Does that horse have no sense?" he demanded. "He will have the bearded men at our heels before we are well started."

"I do not know. He—" Mots-kay began.

"We had better leave him," Pan-sook said with keen irritation.

"No," Mots-kay protested. "I shall not let him make an outcry again."

"Can you prevent it? I remember that from his pen he used to make many such loud noises at the other horses when he could see them."

"I remember that, too, but I shall put my hand across his nose," Mots-kay replied. He grasped the animal's nostrils, closing on them with determination. The horse must not be allowed to give them away. But the stallion kept turning and twisting, trying to wheel about so he could look and listen into the darkness behind.

"Now his feet make too much noise," Pan-sook said. "Maybe it would be best to turn him free and

let him run away. Then the noises he makes will confuse the bearded ones and make it easy for us to escape."

"No," Mots-kay said positively. "I cannot do that. You know of my vision."

"Yes," Pan-sook answered, for Mots-kay had told him of the time when he had climbed the mountain-side and asked his wyakin—his personal god—for guidance. "But," the young Shoshonee went on, "I am not sure all visions come in truth from the wyakins. There are evil spirits as well."

"Mine did. I am sure it can be trusted," Mots-kay insisted.

Though it had been two long years since he had had the vision, he remembered it as clearly as if it had been only the afternoon before. In this vision, a boy walked among the trees of a forest, followed by a horse. The forest was of the Nimapu country, and the youth Mots-kay recognized as himself. He walked easily and with a light step, because his burden was being carried by the horse. That, to the Nimapus (who until that time had seen only a few horses), was the purpose and usefulness of the big animals— to carry the heavy bundles of skins and food when the village moved. Not until Mots-kay had been among the Spaniards had he realized that horses also had the ability to carry people.

But the most memorable thing about his vision

was the horse's spectacular coloring. Mots-kay had never even imagined anything like it. The animal's foreparts—its head, neck, and shoulders—were dark, but its back and hips were white, with a scattering of dark, bluish spots, each about the size of a quaking-aspen leaf. The contrast of colors was startling—so sharp and vivid that Mots-kay would never forget it.

The village elders, when he told them about his vision, shook their heads soberly, and he knew they didn't believe him. But they would—when he brought such a horse among them. And he knew that he would succeed in his mission, because he had great faith in the power of his wyakin.

But during the long months following their capture by the Eutaws, hardships and discouragements had come so thick and fast to the two youths that Mots-kay finally began to doubt his once-strong belief. Perhaps it had not been a sacred vision after all, but only a silly, boyish dream. He now realized how very young he had been—how little he had actually known.

Then, one afternoon in the Spanish compound, he happened to pass by a small pen whose gate was open because one of the Spaniards had gone inside to feed the horse kept there. Mots-kay had never seen this horse before. But when he glanced inside, his heart leaped wildly in his chest. There stood a beautiful stallion, with his head up and his neck strongly arched. It was the *horse of two colors!*

Mots-kay recognized the animal instantly, beyond any doubt. This was the fine, two-colored horse his wyakin had revealed to him—the horse that he would take back to his people, to free them of the burdens that bent their backs and slowed their feet. It was for this that he had been chosen; a great and sacred responsibility had been placed upon him. Now, at last, it was all clear. Everything—the hardships, the disappointments, the long months as a prisoner—was a part of the plan.

Mots-kay was ashamed, then, that he had ever doubted his wyakin, that his faith had ever wavered. For surely none but a great and powerful spirit could have brought him, past all the dangers of such a long and difficult journey, to the little pen and the two-colored horse of his vision.

Now Mots-kay was free, running across the prairie, and the fine horse of two colors was at his heels. Who could have doubts about such a miracle? Mots-kay knew he was not mistaken.

But the horse now was not acting like the same animal that Mots-kay felt he had come to know so well in the little corral. "Come on, Spotted One," he begged urgently.

In reply the horse jerked free, threw his head up again, and sent a strong neigh into the night.

"Let him go! Turn him free so we can escape!" Pan-sook cried out again.

Mots-kay threw himself at the horse's head and once more locked his fingers around the dark muzzle. "No! I cannot," he replied desperately. "I must keep him. But I will not let him make such a noise again."

"You cannot prevent it—he is stronger than you are. He will bring the bearded men straight to us. They will take us back and put chains on our ankles again!" Pan-sook's voice rose in anxiety.

Mots-kay thought a minute, then said, "You go on. Go as swiftly as you can. You know the way."

"Yes, but—what will you do?"

"I shall find a hiding place."

"The noisy horse will betray you."

"No," insisted Mots-kay, "I shall keep him quiet. I shall follow you later. Watch for me."

Pan-sook continued to hesitate. "Come now!" he pleaded. "The bearded men will take you back and strike you with the long whip in front of the other *cristianos*. No horse is worth that much."

"This one is!" Mots-kay shot back, his own voice quivering with panic. "Go now! The bearded men are not far behind. Go swiftly and keep a sharp watch behind. I shall catch up later." He turned back to the stallion, caught the lead rope up short, and said sternly, "Come, Spotted One. We must conceal ourselves quickly."

CHAPTER 2

Pan-sook ran on and in a few strides had disappeared into the darkness.

It was the first time in many months that the two Indians had been separated, but Mots-kay knew that it was necessary. He hoped that this tactic would cause confusion among the Spanish pursuers. Anyway, one horse could be hidden more easily than two.

Mots-kay remembered that a slow-moving, willow-bordered stream lay off in the darkness to the right, and he hurried in that direction. He walked close by the big horse's head and kept a hand on the animal's nostrils, ready to tighten his grip instantly. The horse moved reluctantly and kept trying to turn his head to look backward.

"Stop that!" Mots-kay ordered in a firm undertone. "Come on." He gave the lead rope, tied to the horse's neck, a sharp jerk. There were times, he had learned at the pens, when firmness was necessary.

He gave the rope another strong yank just to let the horse know he meant it.

The stallion then followed more soberly. Reaching the stream, Mots-kay pushed into the blackness of the willows. There he paused to listen, his hand still alert on the bony ridge of the horse's muzzle. The horse sought to lift his head to free it, but Mots-kay held on grimly. After a few seconds the horse became still; but he continued his intent listening.

Mots-kay heard then, too, the pounding of hoofs out on the grassland. The Spaniards had taken time to catch and saddle horses before starting out on the pursuit. Mounted on the horses' backs, they were traveling at a speed that Mots-kay, as light-footed as he was, could not hope to match. How, he wondered, could they do it—ride so swiftly in the darkness and yet keep from falling off? Without question they were brave and strong men, and possessed very valuable knowledge.

That a horse might carry a man on its back was an idea that had not occurred to Mots-kay before he saw the Spaniards riding. Nor had any of his people thought of it, so far as he knew. The Nimapus had strong legs—legs that could carry them anywhere they wished to go (except, of course, the very old and the very young). And obviously, to be so high on a horse's back was dangerous. But

15

the heavy burdens of skins and dried fish and camass cake wearied the people and bent their bones. With horses to carry these provisions, the steps of the Nimapus would be light and easy—like his own vision. . . .

Still there was something about all this that Mots-kay did not entirely understand. Obviously the Spaniards, though they carried no burdens, liked best to ride on their horses, because they hardly ever walked anywhere. Always, on the long journeys, they were carried; even their women and children sat on the backs of horses. To be carried must be a good thing. But the Indian servants—the *cristianos* who accompanied the Spaniards on the journeys—always walked, or sometimes ran, behind the horses or alongside them. Never had Mots-kay seen a *cristiano* on a horse. In fact, it was plain that most of the Indians were in awe of the big, strong four-legged creatures, if they were not actually afraid of them. And the Spaniards tried to make it clear that horses could not be trusted, that they were dangerous. This was something else that Mots-kay did not understand; for it was plain to him that the Spaniards *did* trust the horses and were not afraid of them.

And the horses, Mots-kay had observed, served the Spaniards well—as now evidenced by the steady drum of hoofs out in the darkness. There were four of the riders, galloping across the prairie; and oc-

casionally they called back and forth to each other, in questioning tones. Mots-kay soon recognized these men, from their voices and their vague shapes. One was the thick-bodied man who had been in charge of the corrals and stables, and who had directed the two youths in the work of scooping up the manure and grooming the horses. He was lazy and had an ugly temper. Mots-kay had felt his stick much too often to have any regard for him.

Another was the man whose wife had cooked the food for Mots-kay and Pan-sook to eat. Mots-kay had no feeling toward him—but the woman had treated them kindly, and the food she had given them had been good. He thought now of the food he had saved, which was inside the folds of his baggy shirt. The best thing about the *cristiano* shirts, in his opinion, was the ease with which things could be hidden in them. But he had no intention of wearing one (or the flappy trousers either) to his people's village. As soon as he could get some hides he would make some proper clothes, and moccasins to protect his feet.

The dark shapes galloped on, losing themselves one by one in the darkness. Mots-kay loosened his grip on the stallion's muzzle and wondered about Pan-sook, who was also out there somewhere. The Spaniards, he knew from their calls, had not been certain of their direction or course of pursuit. Doubtless other groups were searching too—made more determined by the outrage that two *cristianos* had escaped with horses.

Leaving the trees at the far side of the stream, Mots-kay selected a course parallel to the water, knowing that it came through a gap in the bench that rimmed the side of the valley. Beyond this bench was rougher ground—ravines and arroyos amid rising ridges. Here there would be a better chance of eluding the pursuers who, he knew, would be searching out his trail as soon as it was light enough to follow tracks. The Spaniards were not fools, and the sign left by the horses would be easily seen.

The stallion kept turning his head to look about in the darkness, but he followed Mots-kay willingly. This pleased the youth greatly. "You are a fine horse, Spotted One," he said—and stretched his stride still more, because not many more minutes of darkness were left. "I knew you were," he added happily.

The sky was turning light when the pair climbed a grassy slope leading to the benchland above the wide valley. At the top Mots-kay paused, wondering where Pan-sook might be. He missed the young Shoshonee who had been his constant companion now for many months. Could he have been caught by the bearded men? Mots-kay hoped not.

The stallion stretched his neck toward a clump of

grass and began to eat. Behind him, across the wide sweep of the bottom prairie, Mots-kay could see a band of feeding antelope and, far beyond, a thin scattering of the white men's cattle, but nothing else of importance. Then he prepared to go on, pulling the lead rope tight.

"Come, Spotted One," he said. "We must waste no time. The men with dark hair on their faces will soon find our trail."

The stallion came after him—but now with increasing reluctance. Having traveled most of the night, the horse was hungry, and he kept slowing down and reaching with his powerful neck for mouthfuls of the grass. This yanked at Mots-kay's arm and soon became keenly annoying—the more so because he knew they were losing precious time. "Come on! We must not stop to eat now," he said firmly. But the horse continued to reach and pull.

After the many weeks of brushing the animal and carrying grass for him, Mots-kay had believed that he knew the stallion well and would have no difficulty in leading him. But now he wasn't so sure. The horse was showing some of the sullen temper he had displayed toward the Spaniards in the little pen. Mots-kay had felt that this behavior had been the fault of the men, for they had teased the high-spirited horse just to laugh at his quick resentment. As a result, most of them would not enter his pen without carrying a whip or stick; and they were well pleased when Mots-kay took over the tasks of feeding the animal and carrying water to him. From the very first Mots-kay realized that this was what his wyakin had intended. It was a part of the plan. "When I escape you will go with me, and I will take you to my people," he had told the stallion softly and joyfully, and the horse seemed to understand.

But now, out on the open benchland in the growing light of the day, the Spotted One was becoming difficult again. He was obstinate and headstrong, not seeming to understand anything nor to care whether they ever got to Mots-kay's village. His only interest seemed to be the grass and he continued to reach and pull and jerk.

"All right," Mots-kay said finally. "You can eat for a little while. I know you are hungry," he added, forgivingly. A frown crossed his face, however; for he could easily see how the stallion's big appetite coupled with his obstinacy could become a serious problem—one that he had not thought about before. Did horses always stop and eat when they got hungry? He had not seen them do so when they were carrying the Spaniards on their backs, but Mots-kay could not be sure. One thing he did know, however; it would not be wise for him to remain there for very long.

"Come, Spotted One," he said firmly a short time later, and gave the lead rope a firm pull.

The meal of grass had obviously helped the horse,

for he lifted his head and followed with a willingness that brought Mots-kay relief and gave him a warming sense of thankfulness. The Spotted One was surely a fine horse—the best of all that the Spaniards had. He wondered why the men had used him so infrequently under their saddles, why they had kept him alone in the little pen. Perhaps it had been because he was a *caballo padre*—a father horse—given special treatment because of the young he produced. In any case, Mots-kay was sure that when he arrived at his village with this beautiful animal, his people would be pleased. They would be quick to recognize the Spotted One for the fine horse he was.

A short time later, he halted on a small rise for another look through the increasing light at the country left behind. Though at least some of the pursuers had passed by him during the night, Mots-kay was certain that, finding nothing, they would circle back to search for tracks. Once they had picked up his trail they would stick to it like leeches, for it would be the quickest way of finding him in that wide expanse. Ordinarily this would not have worried him, because he knew many ways to hide or disguise foot sign. But the deep tracks left by a horse's hard hoofs presented an unfamiliar problem. In fact, he doubted that such sign could be successfully hidden, even from eyes as heedless as those of the Spaniards. His only chance lay in steady and fast travel.

The stallion was already eating again. A fluttering insect made a short, noisy flight past Mots-kay and landed in the grass nearby. Quickly Mots-kay dropped to his knees and, finding the little creature, slapped his hand down on it. It was a grasshopper —an insect with which Mots-kay had been familiar since his earliest days. Now, without the slightest hesitation, he popped it into his mouth, chewed briefly, and swallowed. His people many times had eaten less palatable and less nourishing food than this.

Another grasshopper buzzed through the air and, still holding the stallion's rope with one hand, Mots-kay caught it, too. After he had caught two more, he was lucky enough to discover the grassy nest of a fat gray field mouse. His empty stomach welcomed all of the food he had found. He would save the cooked meat inside his blouse until later, when the problem of finding something to eat would likely be much more difficult. Mots-kay knew how barren and cruel to a hungry person the wild country could be at times.

The stallion still clipped the grass steadily; but something inside himself warned Mots-kay that it was time to go on. He was not certain what tricks of magic the Spaniards might have when on the trail. Many escaped *cristianos,* he knew, had been brought back—and he could not be sure about what had happened to the others. Once, when he had been at the corrals, the soldiers had returned with only a bundle of *cristiano* clothes. Of course these clothes might have been found discarded by the trail. But there was no certainty of that; and Mots-kay had thought that he saw a small, round hole like a smoke-stick made in the shirt.

"Come, Spotted One," he said, giving the rope a strong tug. The horse lifted its head obediently and followed, showing almost none of the nervous excitement that he had displayed earlier.

They made good time across the benchland. The second rise was steeper and was marked by several shallow breaks. Mots-kay made his way to the nearest of these, entered its mouth, and traveled along the dry stream bed. There the earth was baked so hard that even the stallion's hard hoofs left only small sign. Although Mots-kay had no hope that this would throw the Spaniards off the trail completely, he hoped it would confuse and delay them.

Protected from view by the walls of the arroyo, he increased his gait and managed to get the stallion into a trot. They held this pace until the ground before them turned upward sharply again. The climb was over a stretch of dry, tufted grass; and at the top Mots-kay found that he had a long view of the surrounding terrain. Nothing was moving. Mots-kay began again to wonder about Pan-sook. Where could he be? It seemed that the Shoshonee and the dark horse should be visible in all that distance.

Still worried, Mots-kay turned and continued on —a dark, lean figure in his flappy shirt and trousers. The Spaniards did not provide shoes for their *cristianos* and so his feet were bare; but he moved with a strong, light step.

The stallion began reaching and pulling for bunches of trailside grass, and Mots-kay knew he was hungry again. In fact, the horse seemed to be constantly hungry. But his coat, in the early morning light, was bright and beautiful—like the glint of sunshine on shallow ripples. And the spots looked like just-fallen leaves on a sun-washed pool. Mots-kay had known the minute he saw this horse that there could be only one name for him: the Spotted One.

But where was Pan-sook? Mots-kay frowned— because during the recent weeks, whenever they had been discussing their plans to escape from the Spaniards, he had sensed a strange uneasiness in the young Shoshonee. It was as if Pan-sook had had a foreboding of the future, though he had not spoken of it directly.

CHAPTER 3

As the day went on, Mots-kay increasingly discovered that leading the beautiful stallion was not all the delight that he had imagined. The horse not only had a seemingly endless appetite but moreover was surprisingly stubborn and persistent in his demands for grass. Yanking at the lead rope seemed to accomplish little but to make Mots-kay's arms sore and weary. The stallion had a powerful neck.

What the young Indian had not yet learned was that horses, when traveling steadily, need an amazing amount of feed. This is especially true of horses fat and soft from lack of work and exercise, as the stallion was. And having to forage for grass took the animal much more time than he required to eat an armful brought to his pen. It had been many hours since the stallion had last had an opportunity to fill his stomach.

Now the Spotted One gave the rope a vehement tug. Mots-kay knew there was nothing to do but stop. Immediately the stallion began grazing with such evident hunger that Mots-kay could not be very angry with him. Instead, the youth found that he too was hungry; and looking about, he soon spotted a berry bush from which he could eat with one hand while holding the stallion's rope with the other. The berries were dry and withered, without much taste or nourishment. But they were filling, and he ate all of them that he could reach. Afterward he ate a small amount of the cooked meat, taken from the hiding place in his shirt. But this left him far from satisfied; and he said to the horse, "There will be fine camass, cooked to good mush, when we get to the village of my people. There will be the sweet meat of the big fish, too. We shall have all we want to eat." The big fish were the salmon that clogged the Nimapu nets once a year during their run back upriver from the ocean to spawn.

When Mots-kay pulled at the rope again, the stallion lifted his head and followed, though he was still reluctant. They traveled until dark. Mots-kay realized that he was weary, and sat down on a gentle, open slope. Immediately the stallion began feeding beside him. There was one good thing, Mots-kay thought: horses could go without much sleep, which gave them more time to eat. However, he intended to remain there only a short time.

The Spaniards, the young Nimapu knew, usually

halted whatever they were doing when night came, and gathered at the houses where their women had cooked food for them. Then they went to bed, to snore soundly until the next morning. But he was uncertain as to what they would do when traveling. Would they stop to eat and sleep when they were in pursuit of a *cristiano*—a slave who, in escaping, had added the insult of taking one of their fine horses? He waited a while longer; then, though the stallion was plainly still hungry, he got to his feet and tugged the animal onward through the darkness.

Much later, weary to the bone, Mots-kay halted in the dense shadows of a narrow ravine. He knew he had to stop, and he sat down, holding the end of the stallion's rope in his hand. Having watched the Spaniards chase loose horses on the prairie near the settlement, he was fairly certain of the trouble he would have if the stallion got free. But the tugging at the other end of the rope kept him awake, and finally he got up and tied the horse firmly to a tree.

Day was coming when he awoke again. He sat up quickly and looked around. The stallion was still— asleep now on his feet. Mots-kay went to him, untied the rope, and said, "Come, Spotted One. We must go on. The bearded men may not be far behind. Their horses carry them swiftly."

That was of little concern to the stallion. His main interest was grass; and he made this clear by pulling back and reaching for a nearby clump. Mots-kay was thoroughly annoyed. How could any horse eat so much? But then he remembered that the horse had spent a large part of the night tied to a tree. "All right," he grumbled. "But eat fast. Remember, if the bearded men catch us they will take you back to the little pen." He did not want to think about his own fate—but he was sure it would be worse than merely being locked up.

A grove of young pines stood nearby, and among the scattered trunks Mots-kay now saw something that quickly reminded him of the emptiness of his own stomach. It was a medium-sized, darkly colored bird, known to his people as a "fool's-hen" because of its reluctance to take alarm at man's approach. Mots-kay's eyes brightened with keen hope. Quickly wrapping the lead rope about a limb, he stooped and picked up a short length of dead branch. Advancing with slow, stealthy steps, he held it by one end, slightly raised.

The bird pulled back its neck and puffed out its chest, as if somewhat offended by the approach of the Indian; but still it did not fly.

Mots-kay pretended not to notice the fool's hen; but suddenly, when he was only a few steps away from it, he spun about and sent the stick flying. He threw it with a snapping action, so that it would whirl end over end at a short distance above the ground. Not until the stick was very close did the bird suddenly stretch its neck and spread its stubby wings, rising in flight just in time to get into the path of the spinning missile.

Aware that the fool's hen was probably only stunned, Mots-kay leaped forward and picked it up. A quick swing of its head against a tree trunk finished it. Mots-kay reached into the folds of his shirt and drew out the fine Spanish knife, delighted that at last, after all the weeks of carrying it hidden, he had such a pleasant use for the keen blade. Though eaten without the benefit of cooking, the bird made one of the most satisfying meals Mots-kay had had in many weeks. It was almost like being at home, in that faraway country among his own people again. The way there was still long and there were high mountains to cross; but he told himself that he would make it. He would see again the high prairies blue with the budding of the camass flower.

Late in the afternoon, after they had been traveling without rest for some time, Mots-kay felt a sudden tug at his now-sore arm. But this time it was different. Instead of lowering his head to the turf, the stallion held it erect, with his ears turned alertly forward. He let out a loud and abrupt neigh—a sound that battered harshly against the young Nimapu's nerves.

Mots-kay leaped to the animal and clapped his hand over the dark muzzle, but with a fearful feeling that already it was too late. This feeling was confirmed by a quick reply that came ringing down the slope. Turning, Mots-kay saw up there a horse —a big, red horse with a long, tapering neck and lean shoulders.

They had caught him! The Indian stood there, frozen in his tracks, waiting for the Spaniards to shoot him or come striding down and take him prisoner. But no one appeared. Then the horse came down the hill at an eager trot, dragging a length of rope that was knotted about its neck. The Spotted One fought to free his nose, but Mots-kay hung on grimly. Where were the men, and the other horses?

The red horse continued to approach, without fear or hesitation. Then Mots-kay recognized it. It was the Red One—a mare. She was one of the horses usually kept in the big pens, and was reserved for the old gray-haired Spanish priest to ride. Mots-kay, who had groomed her many times, knew that she was calm-natured and gentle—a good horse for an old man. But what was she doing here? The priest had never joined the groups that pursued the escaped *cristianos*.

The Nimapu watched, puzzled and wary, as the mare came on. She nuzzled the stallion. It was plain that the two horses recognized each other and were pleased at being together. Sensing the stallion's contentment, Mots-kay released his grip on the animal's nostrils.

There was no further sign of either Spaniards or horses. Mots-kay frowned, unable to understand this. The horses were almost never alone; surely one or more of the Spaniards were somewhere near.

It occurred to Mots-kay that he still might escape. The wise action would be to abandon the stallion and flee into the brush and rocks, where there were many hiding places. He considered this, then shook his head. No. He would not leave the Spotted One. "Come on," he said to the horse, and gave the rope a strong pull.

The stallion followed readily—and so did the mare, even though her rope was dragging. This concerned Mots-kay and he halted. Trying to escape with one horse was problem enough; and his first thought was that with two, it would be practically impossible. "Stay here," he said softly to the mare. "Go back." Two horses would leave a more noticeable trail and could be seen from a longer distance. Two horses would be more difficult to lead and control. "Stay here," he said again to the mare.

But when he started, on she came again too, her nose close to the stallion's snow-white tail.

Mots-kay paused again, perplexed and annoyed. He did not want the mare to follow him—did not want her anywhere close, because he was certain that before long the Spaniards would be searching for her, and her tracks would lead them directly to him. An idea came to him. He hurried back past the stallion and took up the mare's rope. She stood quietly while he tied her firmly to a small, scrubby bush. Then, returning to the stallion's head, the Indian said, "Come, Spotted One. She cannot follow now."

But before Mots-kay had taken a dozen steps, both horses began to fret and stew. The stallion pranced from side to side, turning his head to look back, and the mare pulled strongly at her rope. An instant later both of them were uttering blasts of dismay, so loud that Mots-kay knew they could be heard at great distances. This, he thought, would never do; it would surely bring his pursuers quickly. Running back, he untied the mare's rope. Though she was an unwelcome problem, he could think of nothing else than to let her follow. Later perhaps he could scare her away—maybe she would run if he threw rocks at her.

But Mots-kay discovered that with the mare at his heels the stallion stepped forward with a readiness that permitted much faster travel than he had expected. Horses, it was obvious, did not like to be alone.

The youth struck out across the wide bench at a brisk walk. No bearded pursuers could be seen to the rear, but now there was no doubt in Mots-kay's mind that they were back there somewhere, following his trail with grim and urgent determination. And now that he had *two* horses, they would be more determined than ever to recapture him. He turned an unhappy glance over his shoulder at the long-stepping red mare.

Mots-kay's face was to the north, where the bright star was fixed in the heavens at night. It was in that direction that Pan-sook would be traveling—if he had not been caught. Toward the north lay the wide, brushy valley of the Shoshonees, though still the distance was great. Canyons and plateaus, and at least two rugged mountain ranges, were yet to be crossed. There were deep rivers too. A shadow of worry passed over Mots-kay's face as he wondered if the Spotted One could swim.

In the middle of the afternoon they entered upon a wide, grassy flat—the dark, lean youth in coarse gray clothing, followed by two horses, one silvery white and the other red. No pursuers had yet appeared behind them, but Mots-kay still kept up his quick stride. Here, however, trouble started, much as Mots-kay had feared.

The mare had grown hungry and began to lag, pausing to gather in mouthfuls of the good grass. Each time she stopped, the stallion halted too, unwilling to go on without her, and Mots-kay's pulling and yanking didn't help much. He soon found that he was losing a lot of time that he doubted he could afford, and this concerned him greatly. He realized he would have to keep the mare moving or else find some way to go on without her. Finally he went back, grabbed up the mare's rope, and gave it a strong jerk, which brought her up beside the stallion. After that, grasping firmly the two lead ropes in one hand, he was able to travel steadily.

In this level land where there was only grass and low bushes, Mots-kay knew he could be seen from long distances—especially with the moving horses. Even the Spaniards could not be expected to miss anything so eye catching. This irked Mots-kay; but crossing the flat was the shortest way to the rougher country beyond. "Hurry! Come on," he called back to the horses, and pulled anxiously on the ropes.

At the far edge of the plain the land tilted gently upward and the brush became thicker, with the small, dark crowns of evergreens showing here and there. Mots-kay kept a cautious watch on this cover as he approached. He was not far distant from it when he spied a movement that brought him to a sudden halt. A gray-clad shape rose out of the brush. Mots-kay had a moment of worry; but this was followed by deep-felt relief and pleasure as he recognized the shape to be Pan-sook, in his *cristiano* clothing. Tugging at the horses, he hurried forward.

"This is good!" Pan-sook exclaimed. "I have been watching for you. I was beginning to think that perhaps the bearded men had caught you."

Mots-kay shook his head. "No. But I am afraid they are not far behind me."

"They are not," Pan-sook told him. "They are only coming to the flat. I saw them from that point of rocks up there." He nodded to a broken rise at the edge of the basin, then added, "They are being carried on their horses."

"How many are they?" Mots-kay asked.

"Three."

"How far back are they?"

Pan-sook glanced at the sun. "It will be dark by the time they reach this place. Why are you leading the Red One?" He did not seem much surprised by the presence of the mare.

"She was back there," Mots-kay explained, "and the Spotted One would not come on without her. I did not want to bring her, but I had to. It must be that she got away from the bearded ones."

Pan-sook shook his head. "They did not bring her—I did. She is the one I got when I went back to the pens for a horse to take to my village. She is the one they always used to carry the priest."

Mots-kay nodded in acknowledgment. "But—?" he queried.

"I turned her loose this morning," Pan-sook said, with some chagrin in his voice. "There was no other way. The bearded men were close behind me, following her tracks. I had to throw them off the trail."

"I am glad they did not catch you," Mots-kay responded. "But now you can have her back." He handed Pan-sook the mare's rope, obviously pleased to be relieved of her.

Pan-sook, seeing this, insisted, "She is a good horse. She is one of the best the bearded men had."

"I know that," Mots-kay agreed quickly. "But it is not easy to lead two horses together. They are always pulling back, or about to step on my toes. Your people will be very happy when you bring such a fine horse to your village."

A shadow crossed Pan-sook's face, as if these words reminded him of something that he did not like to think about.

"What is it?" Mots-kay asked his friend. "What do you worry about?"

Pan-sook squared his shoulders and pressed his lips together in a tight line. "Come on," he said gruffly. "If we do nothing but stand and talk, the bearded ones will catch us before we are well started."

CHAPTER 4

Pan-sook shook his head unhappily. "Why is it," he asked, "that horses move so obediently with the bearded men on their backs, but these that we lead stop and pull in every direction? Do you understand that, Mots-kay?"

It was near dusk, and the two horses had been giving trouble for some time—especially the willful stallion. Mots-kay's arm was weary from all the tugging and pulling. He shook his head slowly and said, "They are very hungry. They need a lot of grass in their stomachs."

"But with men on their backs they must get hungry, too."

"Yes," Mots-kay agreed.

"But they do not try to stop. They do not eat. They do not even put their heads down. I think the bearded ones must know some things that we do not. I have heard it said that they once traveled for many days in big canoes, across water so wide they

39

could not see the other side—yet they did not get lost."

"Perhaps," Mots-kay replied. "Canoes are easier to control than horses." He spoke with the sureness of much experience.

Pan-sook nodded in agreement. "People who live on good rivers do not have a great need for horses."

"But horses can go where there is no water," Mots-kay replied pointedly. "They can carry heavy burdens across the deserts and into the mountains. Upon their backs hunters from my village brought meat and hides from the distant buffalo plains. Canoes cannot do that."

Pan-sook's shoulders lifted in a small shrug; he did not answer.

They had arrived at a small open area on the slope where the grass was especially thick and green. Mots-kay paused, and both horses at once lowered their heads and began to eat.

Pan-sook turned his gaze back to the country behind them and said thoughtfully, "I do not think many Indian slaves have ever escaped from the bearded men—not even those that were not brought back tied with ropes behind the horses."

Mots-kay was slow in answering, because he too had wondered about this. Some of the Spaniards were cruel and unfeeling toward the Indian workers, and these usually were included in the pursuing

40

groups. "That could be true," Mots-kay admitted. "But," he went on stoutly, "they will not kill *us*. We shall not give them the opportunity. My wyakin has revealed that I shall return to my village. You know that."

"Yes," Pan-sook said, "I know of your vision— but there was only one person walking in it."

Mots-kay frowned, not understanding at first. Then he brightened. "Of course. It was after we had reached your home, and I was going on to the country of my people alone. That is the reason only one person was in the vision."

Pan-sook nodded, then changed the subject. "The horses with men on their backs travel steadily. They do not try to stop and eat all the time," he mused again. "It would be good if these horses would carry us. Then we could go as swiftly."

"Yes, it would," agreed Mots-kay.

"But they will not." Pan-sook's countenance fell. "Horses will not carry *cristianos*. You know that."

"No, I do not know it," Mots-kay responded. "The bearded men said it—but I do not know that it is true. I think I would like the Spotted One to carry me."

Pan-sook shook his head. "It would be less dangerous if we left the horses here. Without them we can travel much faster; and without the deep tracks to guide them, the bearded men will soon be lost.

Our legs are strong; and horses cannot go fast in rough country."

There was, Mots-kay realized, much truth in these arguments. Without the horses he and Pan-sook could simply disappear into the brush, leaving no trail that the Spaniards could make out. But his decision had already been made. "Come on," he said, and gave the stallion's rope a firm tug.

It was nearly night when they next halted, in a little swale just under the crest of a winding ridge. Mots-kay selected the spot because of the good grass and the horses began eating with their usual promptness.

Pan-sook sat down and dug into the folds of his shirt for the bundle of cooked meat that he carried. "I wish I too could eat grass. This meat is not going to last very long."

"We shall get more," Mots-kay declared, and got out his own bundle. "We must start looking for good wood for bows and arrows."

"Yes," Pan-sook agreed. "We shall need much meat. It is still a great distance to my country."

"And an even longer distance to mine," reminded Mots-kay. "And there are more mountains that I shall have to cross. We shall have to have robes, and many pairs of moccasins. The rocks will be sharp, and the ground will be hard and cold."

Then they both became silent, chewing on meat

from their bundles. A short time later the youths wrapped what was left and put it away. The horses continued grazing noisily with obvious pleasure. "At least we do not have to worry about food for them," Mots-kay observed, and lay back against the slope to rest.

Some time later, when it was completely dark, Pan-sook suddenly exclaimed, "Mots-kay!" There was such concern in his voice that Mots-kay sat up quickly.

"What is it?"

"There." Pan-sook stretched his arm to point along the slope.

Following the movement, Mots-kay saw a point of light. If it had been above the horizon, it might

have been a star. It took only a second for him to realize that it was not. "It is the bearded men," he said.

"Yes," said Pan-sook. "No one else would build a fire so big that it could easily be seen."

"They have paused for the night. The fire is to cook their food. They always want their meat cooked."

"How long will they stay there?" Pan-sook wondered nervously.

"Until morning, I think."

"Why do you think that?"

Mots-kay shrugged. "I think they are following our tracks. They will not be able to see them again until it is light."

"Yes, that is probably true. But then they will come swiftly, on their horses. It will be very dangerous for us. You know that their smoke-sticks can hit at a long distance."

Mots-kay got to his feet. "We can go on. We can travel in the dark, because we do not have to follow tracks. Come, Spotted One."

With much good grass in their stomachs, the two horses followed compliantly; and the night was far gone before the small procession finally halted again. "We must have sleep," Mots-kay said. "Unless we get some rest we cannot go on, and the bearded men will be certain to catch us."

Pan-sook spoke in a weary voice. "Yes," he said reluctantly. The Indians lay down, both so tired that they were asleep almost at once, despite the slow shuffling of the grazing horses.

Mots-kay was awake at the first light. He lay still for several seconds, listening to the dawn sounds. The horses had ceased to eat and were asleep on their feet. Assured that no danger was near, Mots-kay got to his feet, and Pan-sook roused himself too. "We shall go on," said Mots-kay, taking up the stallion's rope. Pan-sook followed close behind, leading the red mare.

That day they ate the rest of their cooked meat. They stopped only when the persistence of the hungry horses made it necessary. Pan-sook became increasingly nervous and impatient, but he did not again mention that it would be better for them to abandon the horses—though Mots-kay knew this thought was strong in the young Shoshonee's mind.

It was a long, tiresome day. That night, when they halted, Mots-kay was hopeful that they had gained ground on the white men. As the darkness increased, they watched the lower country behind. After a time a spark once more appeared back there, and rapidly increased in size. It was obviously a fire—big and bold after the manner of the Spaniards.

"They are nearer," Pan-sook said unhappily.

Mots-kay saw that this was true, despite their

hard traveling during the day. Occasionally a black shadow that he knew to be a man moved across the face of the fire.

"Their horses move faster than these we lead," Pan-sook went on.

"It is because the men are on their backs!" cried Mots-kay.

Pan-sook's shoulders jerked up. "Perhaps; but it will make no difference if they catch us."

Mots-kay made a decision. "Our horses must carry us, too. Then we can keep ahead of the bearded men. They will not be able to catch us."

"But how shall we make our horses carry us?" Pan-sook wanted to know. "No *cristiano* was ever carried by the horses."

"There must be a way," answered Mots-kay thoughtfully. "It is the things the bearded ones put on the horses' backs and heads—the saddles and bridles. That is the reason the horses will carry them. It must be!"

"Perhaps. But we do not have any saddles and bridles."

"I could make some," Mots-kay insisted. "They are made only of leather and wood. I saw that."

"Yes," replied Pan-sook, "but we do not have any leather. We do not have even hides to make leather. Anyway, there is not time. When day comes the bearded men will be hurrying on our trail again."

All this was only too true, Mots-kay knew. Yet he could not give up—he felt there must be a solution. His wyakin would have foreseen this.

Then an idea came to him. Pan-sook had put it in his mind. "The bearded men have saddles and bridles. They would not come without them. We could get them."

The daring of this proposal almost took Pan-sook's breath away. "How? They would shoot us!" he cried.

Mots-kay shook his head. "No. They will not see us. They must not know of our presence until we are gone and it is too late for them to do anything about it."

"It is too dangerous. We cannot go into their camp. It is not possible."

"Yes, we can!" Mots-kay replied firmly. "You yourself have said that the bearded men have no ears when they are in their beds." He got to his feet. "I shall go alone. Someone must stay here with the horses. I shall get two saddles and two bridles and bring them back. Then our fine horses will carry us, and the bearded ones cannot catch us."

"But—" Pan-sook started to protest, only to have Mots-kay cut him short and press the stallion's lead rope into his hand.

"Wait here for me," the young Nimapu directed, and turned into the darkness back along their trail.

CHAPTER 5

The fire of the Spaniards was in a shallow, timbered valley, near the bank of a small stream. It burned big and bright. Surely, Mots-kay thought, some great power protected people so foolish and careless; and this speculation caused a shiver of concern to run along his spine. But it was not against the men and their spirits that he plotted, but only against their property—the saddles and bridles that he and Pan-sook needed so desperately for their horses so they could escape.

With a final glance backward toward the spot where Pan-sook held the horses in the gloom, Mots-kay entered the valley. As he advanced, a clump of trees hid the blaze from his view and afforded him cover. Holding to the denser shadows he continued on, pausing frequently to listen and look about, his eyes and ears made keener by the knowledge that a mistake here would cost him dearly.

Farther into the valley he arrived at a small open meadow made bright by starlight. He paused for a survey from the fringe of trees. Nothing was visible except for a faint glow in the upper branches of the young evergreens. This told Mots-kay that the Spaniards' fire was in the deep ravine, close to the water's edge. A slight movement of the air brought the smell of smoke to his nostrils.

In the darkness he crept along the edge of the meadow, seeking the place where the smoke smell was strongest. Soon he became aware of a new scent —one he knew well from his months of working at the horse pens. After a cautious pause he turned directly into the wind and advanced slowly, a few silent strides and then a halt to look and listen. A shadow, blacker than the others, moved. Mots-kay was at once motionless. He heard the soft thud of hoofs and recognized the shape of a horse, head down to the grass. Soon he made out two similar shapes not far beyond. He knew they were the Spaniards' horses.

A long moment with his breath held convinced him that there were no men near these horses. He moved forward, his bare feet making only the softest rustle in the grass. There was nothing on the horses —no ropes nor saddles nor bridles. This was a disappointment—though he knew that the Spaniards usually took these things off their horses at night. The saddles and bridles were somewhere nearby, he was sure; the Spaniards could not have come without them. But where?

And how was it that these men dared to leave their

horses untied at night? How could they know that the horses would not wander, or run to escape when approached in the morning? He had seen how difficult it sometimes was to catch horses in the open pastures near the Spanish settlement. Usually the animals had to be driven into pens or corrals.

Mots-kay searched into the darkness under nearby trees, but he could find neither saddles nor bridles. It was obvious that the men had removed them at some other place—probably close to the fire. He came to the lip of the low bank that led down to the stream bottom. Here the fire was in plain view, a short distance downstream. The flames had dwindled to a thick bed of red coals, above which there was an occasional yellow flickering. This faint light fell on a dark, heavily bearded face under a wide-brimmed hat. Reaching out a thick arm, the man lifted a pan from the coals and turned pieces of meat that sputtered in it. The smell of the cooking meat almost made Mots-kay's senses reel—he was so hungry. The Spaniards, it seemed, always had plenty of food and other things that they needed. He slipped down the bank into the deeper shadows at its base.

Two other dark forms then became visible to the Indian youth. The three men ate, squatting near the fire and taking food from the pan with forks made, like their knives, of hard metal. Mots-kay wormed his way forward silently, looking for the saddles and bridles that he was sure were somewhere in the vicinity.

The voices of the men as they spoke to each other reached his ears plainly. He knew them all. One was a young soldier who habitually carried a long gun; he was a sentry on the high wall near the big gate. Another was the burly man who had guarded Pansook and himself, who had shown them how to use the manure shovels and brush the horses. The third

was also a soldier—an older one who wore heavy leather clothing, the front of which was shiny with fat drippings.

But despite the long months of living in the same community with these men, they were still strangers to Mots-kay, and he had no liking for them. He had felt their sticks and heard their angry voices too often. The Spaniards were his enemies—seeking to make him a slave again, to put the hated chains back on his legs as they had when he and Pan-sook first arrived. His freedom-loving nature rebelled bitterly at the very thought, and a new determination that it would not happen boiled angrily up inside him.

Three dark mounds of gear could be seen near the edge of the dim circle of light. These, thought Mots-kay, must contain the saddles and bridles he needed so much—and the thick, folded blankets that were placed on the horses' backs under the saddles. When the fire was dead and the men were asleep, he could slip in, lift these articles silently from the ground, and take them away. That was what he would do when the time came. Meanwhile he had to be patient and wait. This was not too difficult for him; he had already been waiting a long time—most of his life, it seemed.

Then he saw something else, propped against the nearest mound. Long, slender, and dark, with a peculiar crook at its larger end, he recognized it as a gun—a smoke-stick, as the *cristianos* described it. Mots-kay eyed it unhappily, vividly remembering its amazing deadliness—the spurting of the dense smoke and the awesome noise. But he did not intend to let this stop him. The importance of obtaining the saddles and bridles was too urgent. With such equipment he and Pan-sook could ride high and imposingly, like the Spaniards.

The men had finished eating. One straightened and took up a vessel; he spoke briefly and then turned toward the creek. Mots-kay's keen ears caught the word *agua* and he knew the man was going for water.

The two men left lounging in the flickering light talked in low tones, and Mots-kay heard the words *cristianos* and *mañana*. From this he guessed that the Spaniards expected to catch up with the two escaped young Indians in the morning. He realized then that these bearded men must be more skilled in reading trail sign than he and Pan-sook had thought. That was something to keep in mind—because the white men were big and strong and coldly determined.

The third man returned noisily from the darkness and placed the vessel of water on the ground near the fire. In gruff Spanish he asked, "Have you looked at the horses?"

"They are up on the bench, filling their bellies with the good grass," the young soldier answered.

"Go and make certain," the first man directed.

"Oh, they are all right. I put *cojears* on all of them."

The word *cojears* is Spanish for "hobbles." It was unfamiliar to Mots-kay, and he wondered what it meant. He did not remember seeing anything on the horses—either on their heads or their backs. *Cojears . . . ?*

"Go and make sure," the tall man insisted sternly. "If they should get loose and start traveling, we probably could not catch up with them. We must not take a chance on that—not when we are so close to those little heathens."

Loose? Mots-kay frowned to himself. Were the horses not already loose?

"Oh, very well," the young soldier answered, pausing to take a drink from the vessel before getting to his feet. Clumsy in his heavy boots, he came into the darkness, passing by so closely that Mots-kay could have touched him by merely stretching out an arm. The young Nimapu lay very still, listening as the man slipped and scrambled up the low bank toward the horses.

The older soldier got up from the fire, stretched his arms, and walked over to one of the piles of horse gear. "This chasing of *cristianos* is getting to be a blasted nuisance," he grumbled. "I am going to bed." First he put the long gun to one side, then he unfolded the thick blanket that went under the saddle.

After kicking some dead tree limbs out of the way, he spread the blanket on the ground.

Mots-kay watched all this closely. Did the man intend to sleep on the blanket? Mots-kay hoped not, because he expected to take it, too. But he and Pansook could do without the blankets if it was necessary.

The man sat down on the blanket and took off his stiff, heavy boots. Then he stretched out and rested his head, shielded by the dark, flat-brimmed hat, on the saddle. Mots-kay watched this with a sinking feeling. The Spaniard, it appeared, intended to sleep not only on the blanket but on the saddle as well. Why? They did not do that, Mots-kay knew, at the settlement. The saddles were kept on long pole racks in the sheds.

But, whatever the reason, it was plain to Mots-kay that he would not be able to get the saddle. He could not take it from under the man's head, no matter how carefully he moved.

Then, as if suddenly remembering, the man reached out and pulled the long, dark gun to a convenient place at his side. That discouraged Mots-kay still more. While he was thinking about it, footsteps sounded in the darkness behind. He pressed against the earth, his slim body as motionless as a log. The man who had gone to look at the horses slid and stumbled down the bank, then clumped up to the fire.

"Is everything all right?" the tall man asked.

"Of course. I told you it was."

"Did you make certain of the *cojears*?"

"Yes. They are on good and snug. The horses will be right there in the morning. There is nothing to worry about."

The young soldier went to one of the gear piles, spread a blanket, and lay down on it. "We will catch the fugitives," he said confidently. "These *cristianos* have got to be shown that they cannot steal Spanish horses." This man, too, Mots-kay noted, put his head down on a saddle. The Spaniards, it seemed, were surprisingly cunning when they were away from their village—or was it only that they found saddles comfortable under their heads? Mots-kay did not know; but it was plain enough that he would not be able to get the saddles. It would be stupid to try. Perhaps Pan-sook was right in his belief that they could not escape with the horses. . . .

One of the men near the fire turned on his side, grunting loudly with the effort. Another was already snoring.

Mots-kay lay still, keenly disappointed in the knowledge that he had failed. He and Pan-sook would have to go on during the dark hours to put the necessary distance between themselves and their pursuers. They would start again as soon as he got back —for they would need every second of the time.

Cautiously retracing his steps, he came to the foot

of the low stream bank and went up it silently on his hands and knees. Over the rim and once more in the grassy meadow, he straightened, breathing more easily. Soon he saw again the dark shapes that were the Spaniards' horses, one still grazing and the other two now motionless on their feet. He moved closer and paused, wondering once again what prevented the horses from straying. Then the grazing horse took a step—a short stride that in some manner reminded Mots-kay of the way he and Pan-sook had walked when the chains were on their ankles. Could that be the answer?

He moved silently over the grass. The grazing horse had a long narrow white stripe on its head; Mots-kay recognized it as one he had groomed many times. It lifted its head and looked at him suspiciously.

"Wait. Do not make a noise," Mots-kay said softly, holding out his hand. "Stand still."

The horse let him approach and sniffed at his hand. Mots-kay rubbed the smooth, warm shoulder briefly, then slid his hand down one of the horse's front legs. Yes, something was there: it was a strong leather band, and it was connected to a similar band on the other front leg by a thick leather strap. Shackles—*cojears*! With these on his legs the horse had to take short steps, could not move fast or run. So that was the Spaniards' "magic"—not really so mysterious at all!

Another thought then came to him—an idea new and exciting. Could he do it? Yes. Would it be helpful? It might be. The more he thought about it, the more hopeful he became.

Taking out his sharp knife, Mots-kay leaned down and cut the strap connecting the two bands about the horse's forelegs. The horse rubbed its head against his shoulder in what seemed to be a thankful gesture. The Indian took the short length of rope that was about his waist, encircled the horse's neck with it, and led the animal to the other two. They raised their heads at his approach but waited with quiet patience. The sharp blade went through the thick straps between their legs with an ease that made Mots-kay somehow more confident.

The plan in his mind had been developing, and now he thought of a way to make it more likely to succeed. With the rope still about the blaze-faced horse's neck, Mots-kay went on across the meadow. The other two followed, as he had hoped they would, trailing behind in their instinctive urge to stay together.

Reaching the fringe of trees, Mots-kay went into them at about the place where he thought the trail back was. Another opening loomed ahead; beyond this appeared a well-used animal trail, visible even in the dim starlight. Mots-kay set out along this and lengthened his stride. The horses behind quickly showed a new interest in the journey. The trail angled up a slope to the crest of an open ridge, which Mots-kay remembered from the previous afternoon. Here, after a quick glance around, he loosened the rope from the first horse's neck, stood aside, and tapped the animal lightly on the rump. It went forward at a fast trot—and the other two hurried to catch up, uttering soft little neighs of concern at being left behind.

"Go!" Mots-kay cried after them. "Do not stop. Go back to the settlement." He waited until they had disappeared in the gloom, then turned and hurried in the opposite direction—a scurrying, shadowy figure.

It was still dark when the sight of a gray shape that Mots-kay knew to be his bright-coated stallion brought him a warm feeling of relief and thankfulness. He gave two short barks, in imitation of a red fox. The call was answered immediately.

"You were gone a long time," Pan-sook said. "I was beginning to be afraid that the bearded ones had caught you."

"No. They did not know I was there."

"Did you get the saddles and bridles?"

Mots-kay shook his head. "I could not. Would you believe it—the men sleep with their heads on them! It would have been stupid to try."

Pan-sook replied, obviously not much surprised, "They are not so foolish as they often seem. I wish we were a long distance away from them. Perhaps it would be best if we left the horses here. There are some rocks up on the top of this ridge. Over them we can make our trail so faint that the bearded ones will not be able to follow it. Then we shall be safe."

"No," Mots-kay answered, "I think that may not be necessary."

"What do you mean? It is not long now before day will be here, and the Spaniards will then travel swiftly on their horses."

"When morning comes it may be that they will not have their horses."

"But I told you I saw them following us," insisted Pan-sook. "All of them were riding on the backs of horses."

"I cut the *cojears*," Mots-kay explained.

"*Cojears*—? What are those?"

"Shackles. They are like the ones the white men put on our legs, only these are made of leather for the horses. I think it may be that the bearded ones will not be so close behind us when darkness comes again."

Pan-sook frowned. "I do not understand this."

Mots-kay took the stallion's rope and said, "Horses do not remain long in one place when they are free. It could be that the bearded men will have a very long walk in the morning—and we know they do not walk fast or with pleasure. Come. I will tell you about it as we go."

CHAPTER

It was not easy to find a way through the trees in the darkness. But they kept going, and in time they came to the crest of an open ridge, along which they turned thankfully. After this they made better time; but when daylight came, both the horses and the youths were weary from the steady traveling.

Mots-kay slumped to a patch of grass in the early morning light. "We shall have to stop for a while. My legs are too tired to go on."

Pan-sook agreed, and he sat down too. "I wish I knew where the bearded men are," he said thoughtfully.

"Wherever they are, I hope they are walking," replied Mots-kay. "I hope they have not found their horses."

"I do also, but I am not sure of it," Pan-sook said. "They are not fools, and we know how well the horses obey them."

"I am not sure either," Mots-kay had to admit. "As soon as we have rested a little while, we shall go on. The horses are eating; they are hungry. We must take good care of them."

"I am hungry, too. My stomach is hurting because it is so empty. I wish we had some more of that cooked meat." Pan-sook looked around. "We shall find good wood and make a bow. We can make some arrows also. Much food and many hides will be needed before we reach the other side of the mountains. Already my feet tell me that moccasins will be welcome."

"But first we must get away from the bearded ones," reminded Mots-kay. Knowing that he had to sleep, he lay back on the grass and closed his eyes.

The sun was much higher and warmer when Mots-kay awoke. Listening, he heard Pan-sook snoring softly nearby. The horses, having eaten all the grass they could reach, seemed to be asleep, too. Their heads were down, although they were still on their feet.

An eagle floated in lazy circles against the blue sky above, on wide-stretched but motionless wings. The only other sounds were those of small birds and insects in the bushes. Then a staccato burst of noise came from down in the canyon, where a woodpecker was at work on a dead tree. The racket suddenly stopped; but after a few seconds it started again, rising to such a pitch that the rain of blows almost blended into a single long echo.

Mots-kay sat up. Pan-sook's eyes opened, then he, too, arose and rubbed the sleep away with the heels of his two hands.

Mots-kay got to his feet. "I shall climb the high shoulder to find out whether the bearded ones can be seen."

"I shall go, too."

"No. You take the horses and go on. Keep to the ridge. I shall catch up with you after I have looked."

Pan-sook nodded his agreement and moved off, leading both horses. Mots-kay started back along the side of the ridge at a trot. He was annoyed by the flapping of the loose trousers about his legs. The Spanish people, he thought, were very smart about some things, but they did not know how to make good clothes.

Climbing the slope through a stand of tall, straight young evergreens, he came upon a bulky little animal that peered at him from small, dark eyes set deep in shaggy pockets. The creature then turned and waddled away on its short legs.

Mots-kay picked up a stick and ran forward. As he approached, the animal halted, glanced back, and then pulled its head and feet in under its thick body until they could hardly be seen. The hair on its rounded back bristled up defensively. Amid the coat of hair could be seen an armor of longer, yellow spines. Each of these spines was tipped with a black, needle-sharp point. Its tail, short and wide, was also thickly studded with the spines. Now the tail twitched in grim warning to any and all to stay away.

All this was a procedure known to Mots-kay since

his toddling days. That tail could drive a mass of the cruelly barbed spines deep into almost anything it could reach. The movement of the tail was so swift and sure that some people thought the spines were shot, like small arrows; but Mots-kay knew this was not true. The spines simply became detached from their loose roots, from which new spines would in time grow to replace them.

To remove the spines from their target was difficult and very painful. The round, hollow shafts could break easily, leaving the barbed points still embedded; and in living flesh they would dig deeper and deeper. But Mots-kay had long since learned, along with the coyotes and the cougars, that the spines could be avoided—the undersides of porcupines were bare and unprotected. And Mots-kay and Pan-sook needed food.

Standing with his feet well back out of the way, Mots-kay landed a blow on the porcupine's back. This brought a loud grunt, and the creature's head appeared briefly from under the humped, protecting back. Leaping around, Mots-kay laid the next blow on the head. Then, with the animal stunned, the youth grabbed one of its short front legs and flipped it over on its back, exposing the soft, bare underside. A quick plunge of the knife finished the porcupine, and only a few seconds were necessary to open it and discard the intestines and the other parts that Mots-kay knew from experience would be heavily tainted with the bitter taste of the bark that was the animal's favorite food.

Leaving the porcupine there, Mots-kay hurried up to the shoulder, where he scanned the countryside below from behind a screen of trees. A herd of deer browsed on a brushy slope, and not far away he could see the black head and shoulders of a bear that was digging in the remains of a rotted log. On a nearby limb, a dark, long-tailed bird watched the bear's efforts with keen interest; it would, Mots-kay, knew, swoop down to pick up a tasty morsel if one was presented.

No movement and no dark spots were visible along the back trail. The deer wandered into the taller brush, and Mots-kay regretted that he did not have one of the good ram's-horn bows that his Nimapu kinsmen made. Quite suddenly the bird rose and flapped away in disgust. But the bear paid no attention and continued his search for grubs with a heedless indifference that was reassuring.

After a last careful look Mots-kay turned and made his way back along the slope. Coming to the porcupine, he knelt, cut off a piece of the still-warm red meat, and put it in his mouth. It was tough and stringy, as he knew it would be; but his stomach had been sending him urgent signals, so he chewed steadily. Then he grabbed the carcass by a foot and slung it over his shoulder, with the smooth side in.

Finding the horses' tracks near the place where he

had left Pan-sook, he broke into a jog. Pan-sook had traveled with a long stride, and the sun was near its high point when Mots-kay caught up. Pan-sook was holding the ends of the ropes while the two horses grazed. "Did you see the bearded ones?" he asked immediately.

"No."

"How far could you see?"

"A good distance. They are not close, even if they are still following us. Do you want some of this meat?"

Pan-sook replied with a nod of his head—but his manner made it plain that he would have preferred something else.

With their knives they peeled back the thick, fatty skin and cut out bites of the red meat, chewing vigorously before swallowing.

It was not long before Mots-kay had eaten all he wanted. He put his knife away, wiped his mouth with his shirt sleeve, and swung what was left of the porcupine up to his back. Taking the stallion's rope, he said to Pan-sook, "We had better get started."

During the remainder of the afternoon they traveled without a halt. When dusk came Mots-kay turned up a slope to the nose of a ridge, where the grass was good for grazing. Here, as darkness spread over the wide, broken land, they ate more of the tough porcupine meat, then lay back on the ground.

"I do not see a fire," Mots-kay said after a time, looking back down the slope they had climbed.

An owl hooted plaintively down in the canyon, and from the crest of the ridge above came the lonely wailing of a wolf. The stars overhead became sharp and bright, but no firelight was visible in the darkness behind.

"It could be hidden," Pan-sook said. "They might have made it behind a grove of trees or below a cut bank."

That, Mots-kay knew was possible—even likely. He pushed away from him what was left of the porcupine and said, "We need a bow and some arrows. I saw a nice bunch of fat deer today. When we have reached the village of your people," he went on cheerfully, "there will be plenty of food. Your father will be very happy to see you. Perhaps there will be a feast, with many of the white-meated fish to eat." The white-meated fish were different from the salmon that Mots-kay's people ate, and many of the Indians liked them better.

But the sad look that Mots-kay had noticed before came into Pan-sook's eyes. He merely said, "Yes," and turned away. A little later he added, "The Spaniards are very bold and determined, and they have the long guns that can kill at such great distances. There is much worry in my heart. Come, let us go on. It is dark but we can see the star that shows the way."

CHAPTER 7

During the next two days of the journey nothing was seen of the Spaniards, either while it was light or at night. Mots-kay's hope increased, and even Pan-sook seemed to feel better. On the third morning Pan-sook said, "I shall go back. I shall go back and try to discover them, so that we may know how close they are."

Mots-kay agreed. "I shall go on with the horses."

It was after midday that Pan-sook again came trotting up from behind. "I did not see them," he said. "I went back to the high rock above the wide valley, but they did not come into my sight."

"That is good," Mots-kay answered with relief. "If their horses escaped, the bearded ones will have a long walk. And when they have horses again, I do not think they will have the heart to follow a trail so old."

"I hope that is true," Pan-sook replied. Then, holding up a long, straight section of a dried limb, he said, "I found this piece of wood. I think it will make a good bow."

Mots-kay took the limb and tested it in his hand for balance and weight, then nodded. "Yes, it feels like good wood. Keep your eyes open for a piece for me. I hope it will not be long before we have some tender deer meat to eat."

They had not proceeded much farther when suddenly a big, tawny cat bounded up out of a thicket in a shallow ravine whose edge they were following. The Spotted One, in front, uttered a startled snort and wheeled away; but Mots-kay hung to the rope until the horse recovered from his fright. Then Mots-kay looked at Pan-sook knowingly. The big cat had been a cougar. Both of the young Indians had long been familiar with the habits and character of the animal—and this one's muzzle had been red.

Pan-sook handed Mots-kay the red mare's rope and said, "I shall look. Perhaps something is left."

With that, the young Shoshonee dropped over the edge of the ravine and made his way into the thicket. In a few minutes he was back, carrying a big piece of red meat, with the dark-gray skin of a deer still partly attached to it. His teeth flashed in a grin as he looked up, and he called out, "This meat is still sweet, but the cougar ate the good parts inside." Pan-sook was referring to the liver, which the Indians relished raw, flavored by bitter drops squeezed from the gall bladder.

Mots-kay grinned back, and led the horses to the edge of the ravine, where he helped Pan-sook up with his burden. Part of the back and all of the hind leg of the young deer still remained. With no preliminaries whatever, the two youths took out their knives and began cutting strips of the dark-red meat. The keen blades went through the meat easily. As soon as either of them had a strip, he would hold it aloft by one end with his left hand. Then he would take the dangling end between his teeth and cut off the bite with a quick sawing action of his knife. As soon as the bite was chewed and swallowed the whole business was repeated, with amazing speed and sureness.

This went on for some time, while the two horses were giving attention to their own appetites. Then gradually the activity became slower. Presently Mots-kay wiped his knife blade on his shirt front, sighed contentedly, and lay back on the grass. Shortly after, Pan-sook followed his example. Both were soon sound asleep.

The sun was near the horizon and sending smoky golden rays when Mots-kay awoke. After listening, he sat up. Pan-sook was still asleep, and the meat was where they had left it. The two horses stood nearby, heads lowered.

Pan-sook opened his eyes, sat up, and took out his knife again. They ate some more of the meat.

Mots-kay said, "I wish this skin were big enough to make moccasins for us. Our feet need them."

"We shall need many skins," Pan-sook answered. "I hope there are deer in the country ahead of us."

The only food they had the next day was some grasshoppers and white grubs, and a few withered berries so dry that there was little nourishment in them. However, Mots-kay found a piece of wood that he thought would make a good bow. That night, after the day's travel, both he and Pan-sook scraped and trimmed, shaping their bows and tapering the ends. Then they were faced with the problem of providing strings. Pan-sook found the answer to this by twisting together long hairs pulled from the red mare's tail.

"Now," he said hopefully, "if we can just see a deer, we can get some good food. Again my stomach is so empty that it hurts."

It became too dark to see clearly before Mots-kay could finish his bow. He put it aside and said, "I shall go back to look for sign of anything unusual."

Pan-sook nodded, knowing it was the Spaniards that Mots-kay had in mind. That these men might suddenly leap out at them, or shatter the silence by shooting their long guns, was a constantly nagging worry.

Mots-kay went back to a high point and stayed there for some time, but he saw or heard nothing unusual in the darkness behind. "If they are still coming they are far behind us," he told Pan-sook when he returned.

"Or so close they did not think it wise to make a fire," Pan-sook answered gloomily.

They were up and moving at daylight. Mots-kay led the way, keeping a sharp watch for anything that they might be able to eat. Near noon they came to an old swamp, where some dry, straight reeds still stood. "Wait a minute," Pan-sook said. "We can use some of those reeds for arrows." He pushed his way into the growth and began cutting the reeds close to the ground.

The reeds were hollow and light, and the boys fitted sharpened wooden plugs into the forward ends to give them points. Pan-sook tried one in his bow, but it flew off to the left. "We need some feathers to make them go straight," he said.

Late in the afternoon they came to a pond, where a number of small birds were flitting about. Tying the horses, they slipped forward, Pan-sook with one of the reed arrows fitted in his bow and Mots-kay carrying a handful of small rocks, because his bow was not yet finished. Their first tries were misses, and the birds rose in twittering flight. Soon they settled again, however; and Mots-kay and Pan-sook began another approach, crouched and creeping, their dark eyes fixed with the intensity of their concentration. Little by little the birds relaxed their caution, and little by little the two youths crept nearer, combining their stealth with endless patience. Soon Pan-sook was close to a dark, plump bird perched at the top

of a swamp stalk. Beak up, the bird sent out a chirp-
ing call. Pan-sook moved slowly; no noise could be
heard above that of the slight wind in the rushes.
Finally he froze, still in his tense, crouched position,
and slowly pulled back the nocked arrow.

The birds rose again in swirling flight. Mots-kay
leaped to his feet and sent a volley of stones into
their midst—none received a direct hit. When he
turned back, however, he saw that Pan-sook had the
dark, plump bird in his hands.

Quickly but carefully they pulled out the longer
tail and wing feathers. Then Pan-sook split the skin
at the breast and stripped the dark plumage from the
bird. It turned out to be disappointingly small, providing only a few bites for each of them after being
halved.

"At least we now have feathers for our arrows,"
Pan-sook said.

"What we need to catch them is a net like those
my people make for small fish," Mots-kay replied,
still eyeing the circling flight of the birds.

"When they roost tonight, perhaps we can catch
some more," Pan-sook said. "Now we shall fix the
feathers on our arrows."

This was something they both understood. With
the good knives it was not difficult to trim and split
the feathers. Bird blood was used as glue, and the
ends of the feathers were lashed to the reeds with

stripped entrails. Then the arrows were hung to dry.

That night they managed to catch three more birds; and these, inside their stomachs, helped them to sleep more soundly. The next morning, however, practically all of the birds had left the place, and the few that remained were exceedingly cautious. Mots-kay and Pan-sook soon realized that their efforts would be futile, so they untied their horses and went on.

The route was rough and rocky that day, offering no food for them and very little for the horses. Weary and discouraged, they halted late in the afternoon near a grove of young pines. "Perhaps we can find a grouse in those trees," Mots-kay said.

"Two would be better," Pan-sook replied. "Or even another porcupine. I did not know there was such barren country."

But they found neither grouse nor porcupine, nor anything else that they could eat, among the trees; and after the disappointing search, they came back to lie silently on the hard ground near the horses. When morning came neither of them had much spirit or energy, but they got to their feet and untied the horses, knowing that they had to go on. To stay there would be to starve.

Because they were so weak, their movements were slow and they stopped frequently. The hungry horses pulled and reached at every clump of grass. Some dry, withered berries spied by the wayside seemed to increase the misery in the boys' stomachs instead of relieving it.

It was late in the afternoon when Mots-kay, scarcely able to believe his eyes, saw a deer ahead on the barren, rocky hillside. He stopped instantly— and Pan-sook, behind, did also. The deer was young and scrawny, but the image it presented to the two youths was one of beauty. They were filled with eager hope. Pan-sook cautiously took an arrow from his slim bundle and fitted the notched end to his bow-string.

Mots-kay shook his head. "It is too far," he whispered.

"There is no cover, no way to get nearer."

"Wait. Perhaps it will come this way."

"It will not; already it has smelled us."

"Get down on your stomach and try to move closer," Mots-kay urged.

Slowly Pan-sook lowered himself to the ground and began to wriggle forward. He moved a short distance, lay still for a while, then moved some more. Mots-kay, holding the horses quiet, watched with breath drawn.

Pan-sook continued his advance, alternately moving and stopping. The bow and nocked arrow, clutched in his hand, slid along the ground in front of him. Now the deer's dark nose was up and its big ears swiveled, more with curiosity than with fright. Hope increased in Mots-kay's heart. There was a chance, if the deer would just wait.

Pan-sook continued his squirming, moving so skillfully that not a stone clicked nor a dry twig snapped. Now, Mots-kay thought! You are close enough now. But after a long pause Pan-sook crept on, while the young deer stood as still as a stone.

Now—now! Mots-kay wanted to shout. It could not last much longer.

Pan-sook paused again, and this time snuggled down even closer to the hard gray rock. Slowly he began to bring his right hand forward, sliding it up along the side of his body. Mots-kay watched, fascinated, as the hand made its way past Pan-sook's chin to the end of the nocked arrow. Then, still slowly, it began to move backward, bringing with it the arrow and string.

Mots-kay's heart leaped happily. Pan-sook could do it; he was close enough. He would not miss, not at that distance. Shoot carefully, Pan-sook. . . .

Pan-sook was careful, coolly taking his time, pulling the string back and back to give the arrow its needed force. Then, before Mots-kay's eyes, the hand jerked and the horsetail string became suddenly limp.

Painful disappointment flooded up inside Mots-kay. He knew what had happened even before he heard the faint snap of breaking wood. The deer, suddenly alive, whirled and launched itself into a great, soaring bound down the slope. It moved rapidly, and soon was out of sight.

Pan-sook got up from the shale, with a different kind of slowness. The broken bow was still in his left hand. He looked at it with great disgust and then threw it to the ground. Returning up the hill to Mots-kay, he said, "That bow was no good."

CHAPTER 8

During the next two days, moving into even rougher country, the two Indians had nothing to eat except withered berries and two small frogs, which they caught at the edge of a muddy little pond. The coarse *cristiano* clothing flapped loosely about their bony wrists and ankles. They traveled slowly and halted frequently, the weakness and hunger in their bodies displacing their earlier concern about the pursuing Spaniards.

The two horses fared a little better, but the hot, dry winds of summer had also parched the meager grass. "They are very hungry," Mots-kay said once, looking at the spotted stallion's sunken flanks. "This is a bad land. It has been burned by the sun."

They kept going, turning over rocks and looking into old bird nests, searching for anything they could eat. But there was nothing. All the birds and small creatures seemed to have fled from the barren, scorched land.

The two youths did not talk much. There was too much misery in their stomachs. But Mots-kay finished his bow, and Pan-sook found a good length of tough, springy wood to fashion another for himself. "This," he declared after a thorough testing, "will not break." He set to work on it immediately.

Pan-sook too had finished his bow when, upon entering higher, greener country, they came upon not one but three deer browsing in the tall brush of a meadow. Mots-kay halted, and looked again to be certain. Yes, it was true! And already Pan-sook had dropped the Red One's rope and was disappearing into the cover. Mots-kay waited, keeping the horses still.

The deer did not know they had been seen and continued to browse the tender twigs, all the while moving slowly through the meadow. The biggest of them had horns and looked fat.

Mots-kay did not take his eyes from the animals. There stood the food that they must have. The strength was gone from their bodies; Pan-sook must be successful. Minutes passed—long minutes to a youth so anxious and hungry. Then, suddenly, the three deer whirled and fled, disappearing into the trees beyond the meadow.

A little frown crossed Mots-kay's forehead, but his eyes marked the place where the deer had entered the trees. There had been something strange, something frantic, in the largest deer's high bounds. Mots-kay had a hungry hope. As he gathered the ropes to lead the horses on, he saw Pan-sook's dark head appear above the meadow bushes. Pan-sook waved with one long motion, then turned and hurried in the direction the deer had taken. He, Mots-kay knew then, had hopes too.

Finding the sharp, two-toed tracks beneath the trees, Mots-kay followed them; and in a short time he came upon a sight that caused him to sigh with much relief. Pan-sook was standing over the body of the horned deer, having just opened it with his good Spanish knife. He gave Mots-kay a happy look and then cast a brief, proud glance at the new bow, lying nearby on the ground.

They hurriedly took out the liver and began to slice it, still warm, into thin strips, over which they took turns in squeezing drops from the gall bladder. Then they cut off bites of the dark-red meat and stuffed them into their mouths. This was kept up until the liver was gone; then they started on the heart and ate that, too. By the time the heart was finished, their actions were much slower. Mots-kay sighed contentedly and wiped his knife blade on his shirt. "It has been a long time since I had fine meat like that," he said appreciatively.

Pan-sook cut a last small sliver and dropped it into his mouth. "I shall make a fire drill, and tonight we can cook a lot of it," he declared.

"And I shall strip some sinew from the legs,"

Mots-kay added. "This hide will make some moccasins for our feet."

"It should be scraped and worked first," Pan-sook remarked. "That is the way Big Woman, in the Eutaw village, taught me to make moccasins."

"I know," Mots-kay answered. "But we can do that later with other hides. My feet are too tender to wait now. Let us take this meat down to the stream. I am thirsty."

The stream was clear though shallow, and there was grass nearby for the horses. Delving into the cavity of the deer's carcass with his knife, Pan-sook carefully removed the paunch, or stomach, which he then took to the stream for cleaning and washing. Meanwhile Mots-kay cut three short pieces of a stout green limb and, with a big stone, drove them into the ground in a small triangular pattern. When Pan-sook brought the dripping paunch, two thirds full of water, the two of them together hooked the edges over the tops of the stakes so that it was suspended a hand's width or so above the ground.

Mots-kay gathered an armful of small, round stones at the stream's border and brought them to a place near the suspended paunch. This done, he went among the trees, picking up dead and dry sticks and branches. When he returned, he found that Pan-sook had finished whittling a fire drill and was ready to make the fire. With the point in a small hollow on a piece of hard, dry wood, Pan-sook spun the round drill expertly back and forth between his palms—another skill that he had learned among the Eutaws. After a time a small tendril of smoke rose from the dry moss about the drill point. Pan-sook bent quickly to blow on the moss, and the tiny red coal there burst into flame. A short time later the dry wood Mots-kay had brought was blazing briskly.

Using two longer green sticks as tongs, Mots-kay picked up a number of the round stones and placed them in the heart of the fire. Nearby Pan-sook cut bite-size chunks of meat from the deer carcass and placed them on the smooth side of a piece of tree bark. When he had a heaped-up pile of these, he tilted the bark and let the meat slide slowly into the suspended paunch. The water level in the paunch was immediately raised to overflowing.

Then Mots-kay retrieved a hot stone, almost cherry red, from the fire with his green-limb tongs and dropped it into the water. He continued to add stones until the water boiled vigorously, and then kept it boiling by fishing out the cooled stones and replacing them with more hot stones. This continued while the shadows lengthened. Finally Mots-kay took out all the cooled stones and did not put any more in.

The youths then waited with visible impatience for the liquid to cool. Even while it was still uncomfortably hot, they began plucking the gray chunks of meat, dripping with grease, from the paunch. Plopping these into their mouths, the young Indians chewed with expressions of sheer delight. They did not stop until the last piece was gone and the thickened liquid that remained had followed it down their throats.

Only one thing was left to do then, and that was to go to sleep. They slept the sound sleep that comes with bulging stomachs; and the sun was bright and shiny the following morning before they were fully awake. Mots-kay went to restake the horses on fresh grass. Pan-sook took up his fire drill and started another fire. They cooked another full paunch of meat, but this time could not eat all of it. "I think I was beginning to be afraid I would never have enough to eat again," Pan-sook said. "Do you believe the bearded men are still following us?"

Mots-kay shook his head. "Not through that burned country back there. I do not think they have any heart for that kind of travel, even though they carry much food in their bundles." He dropped cross-legged to the ground. "I shall start working on moccasins for us now."

Pan-sook hesitated, then nodded. "I shall hunt," he said. "I can get another deer—perhaps two of them. We can dry the meat and take it on the long climb over the mountains." He picked up his new bow and left.

Mots-kay turned his attention to the deerskin. It was wet and heavy, and the tawny hair on it was thick and straight. He spread it on the ground, flesh side up. Normally the hair would be scraped off and the hide stretched and dried; but Mots-kay's sore feet told him there was not time for that. Putting one foot on the hide to hold it steady, he quickly cut the shape he wanted. For once, he was thankful to the Eutaws for their training.

Wet hides, when drying, shrink drastically, and Mots-kay knew enough to cut his shapes extra big. He cut as much as possible from the neck and shoulder sections, because these were generally stronger and thicker. When he had made four shapes, two each for him and Pan-sook, not much of the hide was left. But Mots-kay decided to keep it anyway; the small pieces could be used for patching.

Forming one of the shapes about his foot, he made a few more cuts to eliminate thick folds and then punched holes, using a sharpened piece of deer bone. Now he pulled sinews from the lower muscles of the deer's legs. The sinews were wet and limp; but he knew, as he threaded one of them through the holes, that they would dry hard and tight. In fact the whole moccasin, which now looked big and clumsy, with the hair on its outside, would dry stiff and hard. But the stiffness would not last long—not with the use he and Pan-sook would give the moccasins. And the hair would wear off quickly wherever it came in contact with the ground. Mots-kay knew very well that they were not the best of moccasins; but he hoped they would last until better ones could be made.

He had almost finished the moccasins when, in late afternoon, Pan-sook came through the trees with a small deer slung over his right shoulder. The deer's stomach had been opened, and Pan-sook carried the liver in his right hand.

"That is good," Mots-kay said happily.

Pan-sook's eyes glistened proudly. He stooped and let the carcass slide to the ground, then urged, "Here, help me eat this liver."

The liver rapidly disappeared. Afterward they made a fire and boiled more of the meat. When they had had their fill, Mots-kay started gathering long, dry limbs. The youths pushed the sharpened ends of some of the limbs into the ground and rigged up drying racks. The racks were skimpy and crooked, but they proved strong enough when they were draped with long, thin slices of the deer meat. Finally, well after dark, practically all of the meat was on the racks.

Then Mots-kay took up the new deerskin, folded it, and carried it to the creek, where he thrust it under the water and weighted it down with stones. The soaking in the water, he knew, would loosen the hair so it could be easily removed from the skin. "I shall make a robe of it," he told Pan-sook. "It will not be very big, but it will be better than no robe."

CHAPTER 9

It was pleasant by the little stream, and both the youths and the horses needed the rest and the good food. Too, there was much to be done in getting ready for the main portion of the long journey. Mots-kay lost track of the number of days they had remained there. Pan-sook, who was an eager hunter, was fortunate enough to get three more deer.

They dried the meat on the racks in the sun, and stretched and scraped and treated the hides to make the leather soft and supple. Mots-kay made breech-clouts for both of them, and they threw away the hated *cristiano* clothing—which by now was so ragged as to be almost unwearable anyway. The Nimapu made pouches, too, for them to carry the fire drills and bone awls and the dried sinew. And there was an extra skin that could be used as a robe, to sleep on or cover with at night.

Pan-sook finally became restless. "Let us go on," he urged. "My mind is not yet easy about the bearded men. Anyway, we must get over the mountains before the cold months come."

Mots-kay was ready to move on, too; so they gathered their few possessions and packed up. The dried meat, by now amazingly decreased in bulk by the processing, was wrapped in the two robes and tied to the Red One's back. She accepted the burden as if it were nothing.

Both horses, filled again by the nourishing grass, followed willingly. Their flanks were once more round and sleek, and Mots-kay found much pride in looking at the spotted stallion. He was a fine horse— big and strong and beautiful. Mots-kay was certain no one had ever had a horse so wonderful.

They traveled steadily, one day after another, on and on through a winding maze of shallow canyons and rock ledges. Although they kept a watch behind, nothing alarming or even suspicious was seen, and gradually they became less concerned about the pursuit by the Spaniards. The bearded men did not like long and difficult trails.

Coming upon a clear, deep pool, the two Indians made a bathhouse by pushing the butts of several long, limber willow limbs into the sandy soil and tying the tops together. This low, rounded framework they covered as well as possible with their robes and the green hides. A fire was made close by to heat rocks, which they placed in a small pit in the center of the floor inside the hut. Then Pan-sook stripped off his breechclout and went in to crouch above the hot stones. Mots-kay brought water from the creek and splashed it in on the rocks, causing white clouds of steam to leap up and fill the hut. The steam seeped out around the bottom and at the cracks in the cover.

A short time later Pan-sook threw back the edge of the deer hide and leaped out, perspiration streaming down his dark, lean body. He shook his head to clear it and then, with hardly an instant's pause, raced to the edge of the cold, clear pool and dived in. His head broke the surface well out from the bank, and his mouth opened to let out a wild shout. The next moment he was swimming with long, powerful strokes. Reaching the bank, he heaved himself up and danced out on the grass. "It has been a long time since I felt so good!" he cried. "I feel almost as though I were back in my village."

It was Mots-kay's turn next. Pan-sook splashed the water for him. The steam swirled up, blinding him and clogging his nose until he could hardly breathe. He felt the sweat pouring out through his skin, cleansing it. The cold pool provided the invigorating shock that he had expected, and a few seconds later he was out in the sun again, jumping up and down on the grass. The blood raced through his veins; he felt strong and warm and vibrantly alive.

90

In the afternoon Pan-sook took up his bow and several arrows and disappeared into the trees to seek, Mots-kay knew, another deer. The young Shoshonee was happiest when he was hunting. Mots-kay untied the two horses and led them into the small meadow, where good grass was plentiful. Watching the animals as they grazed, he wondered again about what it was like to be carried on their backs.

It was an idea that had not come to him until he saw the Spaniards riding. Surely it was less tiring than walking—the Spaniards were clumsy in their stiff, heavy moccasins, which dragged up little swirls of dust as they walked.

Perhaps, too, being carried on a horse was not as dangerous as he had first thought. None of the Spaniards that he had seen riding had ever been hurt— not even the women nor the babies they had held in their arms. On the contrary, the horses had acted patient and gentle. They seemed to understand that they were not to frighten nor hurt the people on their backs. But these people had been bearded ones —never *cristianos*.

Of course, Indians did not need to be carried. They had strong legs that were able to take them anywhere they wished to go. They could travel on foot as easily as horses could, though they could not run so fast. Horses were important to the Indians mainly as the carriers of the heaviest burdens—the

91

packs of meat and hides and camass. But still the thought continued to nag Mots-kay's mind: to be carried on a horse's back looked as though it could be very exciting.

"I wish we had the things that the bearded men put on the horses' heads and on their backs," he said to Pan-sook when the young Shoshonee returned with a small doe slung over his shoulder. "I should like to have the Spotted One carry me, as the bearded ones are carried."

Pan-sook shrugged and shook his head. "He would not do it. Do not forget that you are a Nimapu. Are your legs too old and weak to carry you?"

"To travel on a horse's back may be better than we know," answered Mots-kay.

"How would it be better? I can walk as fast, and with much less noise."

"I could make the things," Mots-kay went on, talking mostly to himself. "I could make the things for the horses' heads and backs. They are made of wood and leather; I examined them in the racks at the settlement."

"I looked at them, too," said Pan-sook. "The things for the horses' backs are called saddles. I saw that they were made of a special kind of wood. It is very hard and strong, and it has a strange shape."

"There is much wood around here," Mots-kay replied. "And we have hides, from which the leather straps could be cut."

Pan-sook continued to shake his head doubtfully. "Only the bearded men know how to make saddles and bridles. And horses try to hurt *cristianos*—you know that."

"The bearded ones said that," Mots-kay admitted. "But I am not sure that I believe them. Why should it be true? Does it make a difference to the horses that the white men have hair on their faces?"

"It must be true," insisted Pan-sook. "The *cristianos* at the settlement always walked. It was plain that they were afraid of the horses."

Mots-kay shrugged the Shoshonee's argument aside. "I shall make saddles and bridles for us," he declared. "I shall make these things, and then we shall learn whether the horses will carry us or not."

The next day, as soon as they had eaten, Mots-kay set out on a hunt for the wood he needed. As he moved through the trees he thought of the challenge of being on the silvery stallion's back—of riding up there erect and confident, as the Spaniards did. If only he could do it!

Mots-kay walked slowly through the wooded area, eyeing branches, limb forks, and broken slabs, looking for a piece of wood that resembled the shape he remembered. Forked limbs, he thought, were the most likely to be suitable, and he considered a number of them. But all had defects, being too large or too small, too old or else weakened by weathering and cracks. Finally he came upon a big fallen tree, deeply rotted on the underside from years of lying on the ground. The litter of shattered limbs caught his eye, and he went among them, looking for a three-pronged fork that might be usable. Then he noticed a piece of the trunk—a round, smooth shell from which the heartwood had long since rotted away. Two thick stubs of former limbs protruded from this shell at what seemed to be about the right distance apart. It did look very much like the wooden frame of a saddle.

Mots-kay took out his knife and began trimming the shell around the edges. Yes, it would make a saddle, when he had cut away all the rotted inside and smoothed it with a rough stone. The limb stubs would serve as the front and back rises—which, he believed, were important in helping the rider to keep his seat.

Back at the camp, he showed the wood to Pan-sook and explained his plan. "I shall carve out the underside until it will fit the Spotted One's back; then I shall tie the saddle in place with straps, as the bearded ones do," he said. Mots-kay began his task at once, cutting away the rotted wood underneath. He found a good rough stone and scraped and rubbed with this. It was hard work, but he kept at it happily. After a time he carried the piece of wood to the stallion and said, "Be still, Spotted One. This will be your saddle. I wish to try it on your back."

The horse arched his dark neck, widened his nostrils, and eyed the piece of wood suspiciously.

"It is only a part of a tree," Mots-kay told him. "It will not hurt you."

Gradually, after being permitted to sniff at the wood, the horse began to show less concern. He had been ridden by the Spaniards, but not much in recent months. Mots-kay moved closer, lifted the wood, and placed it on the strong, white back. The stallion sidestepped nervously and rolled his white-rimmed eyes.

"What is the matter? Why are you afraid of it?" Mots-kay asked.

The horse presently stood still. "There, I told you it would not hurt," Mots-kay reassured him. But the fit, the youth saw at once, could be improved. Taking the slab from the animal's back, he rubbed and scraped some more. After several more trials, he felt that he had done all he could. Leaving the wood on the horse's back, Mots-kay began to cut the straps to tie it in place. The fresh deerskin, wet and heavy, was difficult to manage. Now Pan-sook, who up to this point had been only an interested watcher, moved in to help.

They cut long, thick straps. Mots-kay selected one and fastened its center to the round front knob of the wooden piece. A second strap was put around the rear knob in similar fashion. Drying, he knew, would shrink the straps to hard, unyielding thongs—

which was the advantage in using the fresh hide. Both straps were then pulled tight and tied under the stallion's belly, in the same manner as Spanish cinches. The horse made it plain that he did not like that, though he permitted it.

A third long strap was fastened to the seat of the saddle so that it hung down in loops on either side. "What is this?" Pan-sook asked, touching one of the loops.

"It is a stirrup, in which to place the feet," Mots-kay replied. "Did you not see them on the saddles of the white men?"

"What about the thing that goes on the horse's head? You will need that, too."

"Of course. I have thought of that. Bring me the rest of the straps."

The bridle, Mots-kay found, was easier to make than the saddle—except that he did not have the hard metal part that went into the horse's mouth. Finally he hit upon the idea of using a piece of small, round bone from the deer's front leg for this. When the piece was tied in place, he decided that it would serve very well.

It was late in the afternoon when all was finished. Mots-kay stood back and looked at the stallion. He had to admit that the things he had made were far from being as complete and substantial as the saddles and bridles of the Spaniards, but still he felt that they would work. The Spotted One was wise enough to know that with these things on his head and back he was to carry a person.

"Perhaps it is because our skins are darker," Pan-sook said thoughtfully.

"What is because our skins are darker?"

"That horses will not carry us."

"He will carry me," Mots-kay said. "I shall show you." He went to the stallion and undid the tie rope knotted about the dark neck. Then, remembering how the Spanish riders had done it, he put the strap reins up over the horse's neck and lifted his foot into the stirrup loop, holding onto the saddle knobs with both hands to pull himself up. But suddenly the crude saddle slipped on the horse's back, and Mots-kay found that he had support for neither his foot nor his hands. Letting go of the knobs, he grasped desperately at the silky white coat, clinching it up in folds. Then he knew he was moving—moving faster than he had ever before moved in his life, at a wild, frightening gallop.

"Stop! Stop, Spotted One!" he cried; but that had no effect.

Then he was slipping—falling. There was nothing he could hold on to. He had a terrifying sensation of flying through the air—*bam!*

Lying there on the hard ground, stunned by the impact, Mots-kay remembered what the bearded men had said—". . . horses will not carry *cristianos*. . . ." Now he was ready to believe it. The

Spotted One had been wildly excited and uncontrollable.

Pan-sook's face, wide-eyed with excitement and concern, appeared above Mots-kay against the clear blue sky.

"Are you hurt?" Pan-sook's words sounded strange and far away.

Mots-kay at first could not answer. But after a time he recovered himself, sat up, and looked around. "Where is the Spotted One?" he asked. "I do not see him. Where did he go?"

Pan-sook looked around, too, then replied, "I do not know. He ran away . . . very fast. I think the saddle scared him. It was hanging under his belly."

Mots-kay got hurriedly to his feet. "We must find him—." Then he lost his balance and sat down again, suddenly and hard.

"Are you hurt?" Pan-sook asked a second time.

Mots-kay nodded. There was a dull pain high in his back, where he had landed on the hard earth.

"The Red One is gone, too," Pan-sook said. "When the Spotted One ran, she pulled so hard at her rope that the knot came untied. See, the rope is still there, tied to the tree."

Mots-kay managed to get to his feet. "Look for tracks, so we can follow them!" he cried anxiously. "I must get the Spotted One back at once, or else my wyakin will be displeased!"

CHAPTER 10

The trail of the galloping horses led down the valley through a thick belt of young evergreens and into an open flat beyond. Then it turned away from the creek and angled up a long, gradual slope. Near the top of this they came to a piece of dusty wood in a tangle of deerskin straps. Mots-kay recognized the saddle on which he had worked so patiently. He kicked it aside, wishing he had never attempted to make it.

Beyond this point the trail showed that the horses had slowed to a trot. Mots-kay concluded that it was the saddle, flapping under the stallion's belly, that had caused his wild fright.

A short distance beyond the Indians came upon a dirty strip of hide. "It is one of the reins," Mots-kay said, after a quick examination. "The Spotted One stepped on it and it broke."

The trail led down the opposite slope, into a stand of straight, young trees. Here the sunlight was reduced to long, slanting rays. Mots-kay paused, looking about for sign left by the horses.

"It will soon be dark," Pan-sook said.

But Mots-kay, picking up the trail, hurried on among the tree trunks. Soon they came to the other rein, with the bridle still attached to it.

"Now the Spotted One has no wood nor straps on him," Pan-sook remarked. "Why don't they stop? Where are they going?"

Mots-kay shook his head. "I do not know, but we must catch them." He increased his gait to a limping trot.

But when night arrived, the horses were still not in sight. Finally, no longer able to follow the tracks in the dark, Mots-kay halted. "We shall have to wait until morning," he panted.

"Our belongings are back there," said Pan-sook; and they began to retrace their steps through the darkness. Mots-kay was moodily silent. When they reached the camp Pan-sook gathered dry wood and made a fire. They cooked some meat and ate it. Then Pan-sook lay back to sleep—but Mots-kay began gathering his few possessions. "I want to travel now, as far as we can," he told his friend. The young Shoshonee, with a sigh, got up and gathered his own things.

But when they set out, Mots-kay found that his left leg was so sore he could hardly walk. They had to stop on the crest of the ridge above the creek. The next morning they went on, but because of Mots-kay's leg they made only slow progress. Mots-kay fretted and fumed unhappily. Late in the afternoon he turned and said to Pan-sook, "You go on ahead and find them. Try to get your rope on the Red One; the Spotted One will not go on without her. I shall follow as fast as I can."

Mots-kay rested a while, then continued on when the pain in his leg had lessened. He had reached the wooded valley when, just before dark, he saw Pan-sook returning. "I did not see them," Pan-sook reported glumly. "Perhaps we cannot catch them. Unless we turn back, the deep snow may find us on this side of the mountains."

Mots-kay considered this and admitted the truth of it—but he shook his head firmly. "I must have the Spotted One. I cannot go without him; my vision has shown it. I am sure we shall catch up with him tomorrow."

They started again at daylight the next morning. The tracks were clear and fresh. Mots-kay's leg was better, and he followed them with a quick, eager stride, realizing now that the stallion had become the most important thing in his life.

The sun sent its bright, warm rays across the rolling plain. The youths entered a wooded area where the sign showed that the horses had stopped to graze.

Then, a little farther on, there was a marked change. Mots-kay halted, frowning. "They are running again. Why is that?"

Pan-sook examined the widely spaced prints and shook his head. There seemed to be no explanation for it. The Indians quickened their stride, eyes intent on the hoof tracks.

Some time later, crossing a sandy bottom, Mots-kay halted abruptly with a surprised grunt. "What is it?" Pan-sook asked, coming up from behind.

Mots-kay pointed to the sand, where there was the clear, sharp imprint of a human foot. And beyond

this one was another, directly next to a round hoof mark.

Pan-sook's eyes widened. "A man has been here!" The hoof track, both of them knew well, had been left by the Red One's right front foot.

Mots-kay dropped to a crouching position, then lifted his gaze and swiftly swept it over the country before them.

"It is a Eutaw," Pan-sook said, crouching too. "I made enough of their moccasins when I was a slave to know the mark they leave."

It was a big track, left by a strong foot, the toes turning slightly inward. Mots-kay nodded, then stood up and went quickly along the wash, his eyes sweeping the ground. "There are more than one. I believe they saw our horses and are following them. They will try to catch them."

"That is likely," Pan-sook answered. "We know how eager the Eutaws are for horses. I have had bad dreams about the Eutaws. I do not want to fall into their hands again."

"Nor do I," Mots-kay agreed heartily. His previous experience with these Indians had been that of cruel treatment and helpless humiliation. He climbed to the rim of the wash and studied the land around them, his dark, lean face deeply troubled.

"We can head directly for my village," Pan-sook said. "My people will welcome us. And they will give you food and the things you need for the journey on to your home."

Mots-kay thought about that, then slowly shook his head. "No. I cannot. I must not leave the Spotted One. You know the reason."

"But you do not have him," Pan-sook answered. "How can you get him again? The Eutaws are in front of us. They are fierce fighters. There is great danger—I am sure of it."

Mots-kay continued to shake his head. "I must have him again. There will be some way."

"What way? The Eutaws are not so foolish as not to know what is going on in the countryside about them. And it may be that we are not far from one of their villages."

"The Spotted One has no confidence in strangers," Mots-kay replied hopefully. "He will run from them. Perhaps they cannot catch him."

"They will. They will catch him." Pan-sook knew the Eutaws too well to have any doubts as to that.

"But it will take time," Mots-kay insisted. "It will not be easy for them. Perhaps we can get to him first, if we try hard. We can travel at night and make our way around the Eutaws."

A shake of Pan-sook's head showed that he had little faith in that idea. He said, "They will see our tracks. They will know we are there. You know what will happen then. They will be after us as eagerly as they are after the horses. Then all we can do is run—for our lives. Are horses worth so much?"

Mots-kay considered the question soberly, then answered, "Yes. The Spotted One is. My people have been waiting for his coming for many moons now. He will be of great importance to them."

He turned then, to set out on the trail. Despite his dogged determination, Mots-kay did not underestimate the dangers that lay ahead. He knew that the Eutaws were all that Pan-sook had said they were. But an inner force greater than fear drove the young Nimapu on.

They traveled slowly, taking advantage of any opportunities for concealment and carefully scanning the terrain ahead. Memories of the previous time they had trailed Eutaws were still sharp and clear in their minds, for it was then that they had blundered into the ambush that had resulted in their capture.

Pan-sook murmured, "My mind is uneasy about this."

In another bare area the tracks showed even more clearly. Mots-kay paused to study them. "I think they are six," he said. "One is carrying a long stick—likely a spear such as we saw in their village."

"All are men," Pan-sook added. "It is a war party, looking for a fight or for something they can steal. If they were only hunting, their women and children would be with them. It will not be good for us if they learn we are here."

"No," Mots-kay had to agree. "We must be very careful."

"And how can we be careful if we are in front of them, as you plan?" Pan-sook asked bluntly.

Mots-kay said, "Perhaps they will get tired and will quit the trail."

"You know them better than that," retorted Pan-sook.

"They do not have any pens," persisted Mots-kay. "The Spaniards always caught their horses by running them into pens. You saw that."

"Yes, I saw it. But the Eutaws will find some way, given time. You can be sure of that."

"The Spotted One is wise, and he can run fast."

"How do you expect to catch him, even if we get ahead of the Eutaws?" Pan-sook asked pointedly.

"I can," Mots-kay answered confidently. "I know him, and he knows me. I shall be calm and move slowly; he will understand that I will not hurt him. Running excites horses, and it is not good to excite them. That is something I learned from watching the herds at the settlement."

"But first," reminded Pan-sook, "we must get ahead of the Eutaws."

Mots-kay nodded and said, "Come on."

The trail wound deviously through the ravines and

over the ridges, showing that the horses had traveled with the single purpose of keeping away from their pursuers, who obviously had been in sight of them. The moccasin tracks kept faithfully to the hoof prints of the horses, blotting them out in places.

At a waterhole, cleanly lined hoofprints in the mud showed where the two horses had stood side by side to drink. Handprints were there too—at the water's edge, where the men had lain. Mots-kay noticed that in one such print a finger was missing. "This one is tall," he said, measuring the distance from the hand to the toeprints with his eyes. Moving along the bank, he studied other signs. "I think they are a long distance from their village, for they have robes and pouches and extra moccasins." He pointed to light marks on the ground.

The two youths drank there, too, then found the tracks leading away and set out after them. Mots-kay's courage grew and he increased the pace, reasoning that the Eutaws would be too engrossed with the prize ahead of them to pay much attention behind.

The trail turned onto a rolling plain, and a short time later they briefly glimpsed the Eutaws ahead as the party went over a low crest. The shapes were dark and vague in the twilight. Mots-kay stretched his stride still more. When darkness came the two boys had also cleared the crest; but the trail stretched on to an unseen end. There was nothing to do but halt for the night. They ate some meat and lay down on their robes.

The next morning they started again. The tracks were easy to follow, but neither the horses nor the men could be seen. They traveled at a steady pace all day, following and hoping. Once, near the middle of the day, they could see distant figures ahead. The horses, Mots-kay noted thankfully, seemed to be well in front of the men. Later in the afternoon they came upon a discarded moccasin, evidently thrown aside because of a hole in its bottom. Neatly sewn with sinew, it was the work of a skilled woman—or of a well-trained slave such as they had been. Mots-kay dropped this moccasin into his pouch; even with the hole, it might easily prove more useful than one of his own after a few more days of such travel. But he took some comfort in realizing that even with their winding and turning, the horses were taking him and Pan-sook in the general direction of the wide valley of the Shoshonees.

Still later that same afternoon they saw the men again: six dark-skinned figures wearing breechclouts and carrying robes and pouches. This time they were so near that Mots-kay quickly sank into the protection of the low brush. Pan-sook dropped down also, then crawled up to a position beside Mots-kay.

"Where are the horses?" Pan-sook whispered. "I do not see them."

"Over the rise, most likely. Anyway, the Eutaws

have not caught them. I told you that the Spotted One is wise and crafty."

"Yes."

"Tonight we shall circle in front of the Eutaws," Mots-kay said. "If we stay to one side, they will not see our tracks."

The first deep shadows of night had come when they topped the crest. Mots-kay paused to study the land below. It was a small valley, with tree-bordered stream winding along its bottom. Otherwise not much could be seen in the gathering gloom. After listening intently for some time, the two youths started down through the darkness. They moved slowly, cautiously. Mots-kay could feel the cold presence of danger in the soft night breeze. Little shivers ran between his shoulder blades.

Then, he smelled the smoke! The two young Indians halted, standing perfectly still, alert and tense. The breaking of dry sticks sounded below, surprisingly close. A faint glow soon showed against the sides of the bushes ahead. The glow became stronger and brighter, and sparks appeared, shooting upward into the night.

Suddenly a ghostly figure came out of the dark and stood in the firelight, tall and dark, the muscles of his arms and chest rippling under the glint of an oily skin. He had a strong, sharp nose and a wide, thin-lipped mouth.

110

Mots-kay began backing away, slowly, feeling out each step. Pan-sook silently did the same. It was not until they were well back up the slope that Mots-kay dared to speak. "We can get around them now," he said in a guarded whisper.

When they had reached a point well above the Eutaws' camp, they again turned downward until they came to the shallow creek. They waded across, stepping carefully to reduce the splashing noise. On the far bank Mots-kay paused and listened, his keen ears attuned to the crisp night. Hearing nothing disturbing, he motioned Pan-sook on up the opposite slope. At last he turned to his Shoshonee friend with a pleased whisper: "Now we are ahead of them."

Pan-sook's answer was a question. "Where are the horses?"

"We shall have to wait. When it is light I hope we can find them."

It was still a long time until dawn. Finding a dense clump of low brush, the youths crawled in under the lower limbs. "We can sleep here without being afraid," Mots-kay whispered.

But because of the tense feeling inside him, Mots-kay awoke several times during the night. Each time he listened carefully in the darkness; but there was nothing except the musical howling of the little prairie wolves.

When the new day began to push up into the edge

of the sky, Mots-kay was again awake. So, too, was Pan-sook. They peered eagerly through the branches as the gray early light spread over the earth and the extent of their vision increased. Then Mots-kay felt a touch on his shoulder; Pan-sook, with a slight movement of his eyes, was indicating the slope to their right.

Mots-kay nodded with a sudden, fierce happiness as he made out two shapes, one silvery in the new light and the other darkly red. There could be no mistake—it was their horses, grazing hungrily on the slope. Hope leaped in Mots-kay's breast. He could catch the stallion now; he was sure of it! And in a very short time they would be over the crest and out of sight.

Again there was a touch on Mots-kay's shoulder, and this time Pan-sook's look indicated the creek bottom below them. Mots-kay's hopes fell to the pit of his stomach. There, standing among the bushes, a tall, dark form was stretching long, sinewy arms above his head. While Mots-kay watched, a second man pushed up into sight. The Eutaws were already awake.

CHAPTER 11

One of the Eutaws spun a fire drill between his palms to start a blaze. When it was going, he put on a few pieces of dry wood. Another man took a deer paunch to the creek and dipped it into the water. Carrying it back half full, he hung it between three stakes. He then repeated the procedure with another paunch. Meanwhile one of his companions chopped a big piece of meat into small chunks, using a stone-headed hatchet.

Soon steam was rising from the paunches. As the men waited for the water to boil, two of them twisted long strips of rawhide into what obviously was to be a rope. From time to time one or another of them would lift his head to look at the two horses feeding on the slope. Though Mots-kay knew that the horses could not be unaware of the men below, the two animals seemed calm, showing no concern.

Finally the tall Eutaw, who evidently was the group's leader, went to one of the paunches and, with a quick, two-fingered dip, took a chunk of meat from the hot liquid. He tossed the meat into his mouth and began to chew. Soon all were eating, gathered in two small groups about the smoking paunches. Though they watched the horses frequently, they did not seem to be in any particular hurry; and this puzzled Mots-kay. If they had been trying to wear the horses down by running, why were they permitting them to eat and rest now?

The six Eutaws had black hair that spread back from their foreheads, and their upper bodies were lean and coppery. They wore leggings and breechclouts. Robes and pouches as well as extra moccasins were lying about in the small clearing. The group's bows and arrows were in good fringed hide cases.

The men finished eating, took the paunches off the stakes, and passed them around, drinking the remaining liquid. Then four of them got to their feet. Two went downstream and two up, one man of each pair carrying a rope. They disappeared from sight in the bushes.

Mots-kay looked at Pan-sook, a puzzled frown in his eyes. Pan-sook shrugged, indicating that he did not understand either.

The remaining two men, one of whom was the tall leader, continued to squat near the fire on their haunches, talking in low tones and watching the grazing horses.

Time passed. Mots-kay and Pan-sook lay still and alert in their thicket, not daring to move. Their position, Mots-kay thought to himself, was much closer to the Eutaw camp than he had planned.

The silvery stallion lifted his head and glanced questioningly at the crest of the ridge behind; the mare ceased eating, too. At the fire the two men rose. One of them held a rope. The other—the leader—carried a short battle lance, made of dark, polished wood and with a small stone point. They separated after moving a short distance along the stream bank, then waded through the shallow water.

Immediately the stallion wheeled to face them, his head high and his trim, dark ears alert. The mare moved close to his side and lifted her head to gaze across his withers.

Widening the distance between themselves still more, the two men breasted the grassy slope and began a steady advance upward. This was a maneuver the horses seemed familiar with, because they turned and started for the crest, the red mare trotting in front. Suddenly she stopped. Her long, tapered neck arched suspiciously. The stallion halted too, as at the crest a dark figure rose from the grass to full height.

Instantly the stallion turned sharply to the right and increased his gait to a high trot. A second man appeared in his path and lifted his arms in a blocking

115

gesture. The stallion turned still more to the right and broke into a gallop, the mare keeping close to his side. But now another figure was before the horses; and a fourth appeared presently, completing a surrounding circle. What the Eutaws had planned was plain enough now.

The Spotted One reared, pawed briefly at the air, and spun about frantically on his hind feet, seeking a way out. But everywhere he turned, the dark men shifted to confront him, throwing up their arms in a threatening manner. At last the stallion halted; and the red mare, snorting her excitement, crowded close to his gleaming flank. They stood together, the stallion tossing his head sullenly.

The two men on the crest edged downward while those on the sides moved in, openly and boldly. The tall leader and his companion came up from the bottom, gradually tightening the circle.

The spotted horse made a half turn and sent out a shrill neigh of mixed resentment and concern. He pawed the ground with two quick strokes, then dashed at an opening. But two of the men leaped quickly toward each other, closing the space. They shouted and waved their arms, and one of them sent the end of a rope snaking through the air.

The stallion's hard hoofs threw up a spray of small stones as he wheeled toward another opening. Again the men jumped to turn him back. Spinning

116

about, the stallion bumped into the mare, who was tossing her head in wild panic. They surged against each other inside the closing circle of leaping, shouting men. The stallion darted swiftly at a small opening, but another man leaped in front of him, waving skinny, dark arms.

This time, however, the silvery horse did not retreat. His head shot forward, dark ears flattened against his arched neck. His jaws snapped open. The man uttered a shrill cry of fright as the rows of heavy, yellow teeth closed on the flesh of his naked shoulder. The Indian was lifted free of the ground, and then the stallion's charging knees knocked him violently to his hands and knees. He staggered blindly up just in time to receive a full blow from the leaping mare's shoulder. When the man stopped rolling he lay very still. The two horses raced over the crest and out of sight.

Mots-kay looked at Pan-sook. The young Nima-pu's eyes were wide with wonder and excitement—and proud approval, too. "Did you see?" he asked in an awed whisper.

Pan-sook nodded vigorously, his own eyes gleaming with pleasure.

The Eutaws danced a second longer in a bitter frenzy of disappointment and shouted loud threats in the direction of the vanished horses. Then the tall leader turned back down the slope, thumping the ground angrily with the butt of his lance as he strode along. Two of the Indians went to the injured man, who lay still for some time. When he did rise, it was with slow and painful movements. He held one hand clamped to his shoulder, and one leg seemed unable to bear his weight. The other men kept him from falling.

The dark men straggled down the slope, crestfallen and silent. They splashed carelessly through the water to the smoking embers of the fire. The tall leader threw himself down on a robe, and the injured man was lowered to another robe, where he lay with eyes closed, evidently in pain.

The Eutaws remained by the fire for some time, plainly undecided. Mots-kay, watching from the thicket, began to have hopes that they would now give up and go back. But then the tall leader bounded to his feet and glared around. He spoke in loud, challenging words that Mots-kay and Pan-sook could hear, in the language now almost as familiar to them as their own tongues.

"We can catch them!" the leader declared angrily.

"They are very tired. They will not be able to take many more days of running. Come with me, and I promise that we shall put our ropes around the big white stallion's neck. We shall catch the red mare, too. The spirits have given us this great opportunity to get two fine horses. Who will go with me?"

One of the others spoke in lower tones, nodding toward the injured man.

"You stay here with him," the big leader replied. "Stay with him until he can travel, then follow after us. If too much time has passed, then go back to our village. We shall take the horses there. Our people will sing our praises when they see what fine animals we have brought."

The other three men stirred and began gathering their possessions—bow cases, pouches, robes, and ropes. The leader, resting his short lance lightly on the ground, waited until they were ready. Then the four of them waded across the stream. In a tight little group they went up the slope, over the top, and on out of sight. The fifth man watched until they were gone, then put sticks of fresh wood on the bed of coals. The injured man did not move.

Pan-sook looked at Mots-kay and shrugged helplessly, knowing well that this was not a favorable development for the two youths. Mots-kay's lips tightened grimly.

The sun swung upward in its path across the sky.

The Eutaw tending the fire below carried a paunch to the water and brought it back half filled. Soon it was bubbling between the three stakes. The injured man turned on his side and dragged himself to a place in the shade, where he slumped back to the ground and lay still.

The other man went to the steaming pouch and snatched a chunk of meat out of it. He ate, squatting on his lean, dark haunches. Afterward he took some food to his companion, who managed to prop himself on one elbow to eat.

Mots-kay touched Pan-sook, motioned, and began to back slowly out of the thicket on his stomach. Pan-sook followed, equally silent. When they were clear of the branches they began to crawl up the slope, keeping the thicket between them and the camp. A short time later they were over the top.

"Now there are Eutaws both in front of us and behind us," Pan-sook said, his eyes solemn.

Mots-kay saw the discouragement that had been coming more and more frequently to Pan-sook's face. He attempted to lighten his friend's mind. "Did you see how the Spotted One fought?" he asked.

Pan-sook nodded. "Yes. He will not be easy to catch."

"Yes, he will—for us!" Mots-kay insisted. "He knows me; he will let me approach. I do not think these Eutaws have had many horses, or they would know that shouting and running and throwing ropes only makes them harder to catch. Come on."

Pan-sook hesitated and looked longingly to the north, in the direction of his village, before he followed.

The tracks, easily seen, led down the slope and out across another valley to its timbered bottom. There, in the open soil under the trees, the imprints of both hoofs and moccasins were clear. Mots-kay slowed his long stride, peering carefully ahead.

Beyond the trees the trail entered upon a wide, grassy area. Here the horses had cropped a few mouthfuls of grass. Farther along, the two tracks separated; the prints of the hoofs continued straight ahead, while the moccasin prints angled to the right. Mots-kay kept to the hoof tracks, but they had not gone much farther when these, too, turned sharply to the right.

"The Eutaws can see the horses again," Mots-kay said. "They cut across to shorten the distance. The horses do not run very fast or very far anymore." A look of troubled concern came into his eyes, because the reason was plain. The horses were tired—too tired to maintain their former vigilance and caution.

Soon they found that the moccasin tracks rejoined those of the hoofs. Not far beyond that, a noticeable difference in the hoof tracks appeared. "The horses were running again here," Mots-kay said, pointing to the longer strides.

Pan-sook nodded. "The Eutaws were running, too. Perhaps they thought they were about to catch the horses."

"We can also run," Mots-kay declared, and increased his gait to a jog.

In the distance could be seen several flashing white spots. Pan-sook knew well what they were: antelope sending danger signals by erecting the patch of white hair on their rumps. "I wish we had one of those fat antelope," he said. "All of my meat is gone."

"We cannot stop now," answered Mots-kay, without slowing his steady pace. "We are close behind the horses. When we catch them we shall head straight for the wide valley that is the home of your people. I do not think the Eutaws will follow us many days in that direction."

"It is a good plan. But no one can say what these Eutaws will do," Pan-sook grunted. "I wish we were out of their country."

Dusk came, and yet they had not sighted the men and animals ahead. It was soon too dark to follow the tracks. Mots-kay halted, straining his eyes into the night. "They are there somewhere," he insisted. Then he made a decision. "We shall go around them again."

It was difficult in the darkness—difficult and dangerous, because of the possibility that they might blunder onto the Eutaws. Also, they did not know whether the trail continued straight ahead or turned aside. Aware of this possibility, Mots-kay and Pan-sook made a wide semicircle through the gloom of the early night. They were silent and cautious; but nothing unusual was seen or heard. Presently a rounded knob of land could be seen against the lighter sky. Mots-kay turned toward it. When they had reached the top, he said, "Let us wait here till morning. We should be able to see the horses from this rise."

Pan-sook offered no objection; whatever his thoughts, they were kept to himself.

They pulled their light robes close about their shoulders and lay down on the dry grass. Neither of them mentioned their empty stomachs, but Mots-kay knew that they could not go much longer without food of some kind. Perhaps the spirits would grant them good fortune the next day.

He was awake with the first light of morning, and Pan-sook came to crouch at his side. The knob, they could soon see, was only a higher point on a crooked ridge. Below them was a shallow but fairly wide valley, bare of trees except those that bordered a winding stream. They searched the country carefully with their eyes—but the hoped-for white and red forms were not to be seen.

Mots-kay frowned, worried that his maneuver might prove to have been a mistake. The horses, he knew, could have turned aside at many places. If they had, the only thing left to do would be to go back and find the trail again. This would cost them valuable time. And still more time would be needed to hunt for food. Mots-kay was so tired and so hungry that a feeling of hopelessness began to have its way inside him.

Then, from around the bend in the valley to the left, the two horses came into view.

CHAPTER 12

Mots-kay jabbed Pan-sook with a forefinger, to direct his attention downward. Pan-sook responded with a pleased nod. Raising himself slightly from his prone position for a better view, Mots-kay wondered what way would be best to go about catching the animals.

The Red One was in front. Mots-kay saw that they were moving at hardly more than a walk. As the two horses came closer, he realized that they were heavily weary and footsore. The silvery stallion limped visibly every time his right forefoot struck the ground.

But as Mots-kay prepared to get to his feet, Pan-sook touched him in silent warning. Looking back at the bend, Mots-kay saw another figure—a man, wearing moccasins, leggings, and a breechclout.

The young Nimapu's eyes turned dark with bitter disappointment, and he flattened himself to the earth. As the man came on, Mots-kay noticed that he carried a short spear lightly balanced in his right hand. Then, behind him, another dark figure appeared— and still another—and, finally, a fourth. They were the Eutaws, of course—closer now, and matching the speed of the horses stride for stride. Mots-kay hated them for their successful pursuit.

On came the little procession of weary horses and men. The distance between them, however, seemed to stay the same; and as they passed under the knob, Mots-kay could see that the Indians, too, were heavy footed and slack mouthed. Suddenly the last man fell heavily into the dust. Those in front pounded on doggedly, giving no evidence that they were aware of it. The man lay still for a few deep, gasping breaths, then pushed back to his feet and continued on, following the others. He was the last to go out of sight around the upper bend.

"We shall follow them," Mots-kay declared. "The Eutaws have not caught up yet. And if they do catch the Spotted One, I shall steal him back. I shall follow them to their village if necessary!" His voice was shrill with resentment and desperation.

Pan-sook was silent for a moment, considering his friend's outburst. Then he got to his feet. "Come," he said. "It is time we started." And he led the way down the slope.

Mots-kay usually had been the one in front during the chase. But now, in his mood of sore disappointment, he gratefully yielded direction to the young Shoshonee. And, despite his weariness and hunger, Pan-sook struck a trot as soon as they reached the valley floor.

The trail was so fresh that they could follow it with only brief glances now and then. Pan-sook stayed in front and kept their jogging pace steady. Mots-kay ran as lightly as he could, seeking to save his strength.

A sudden, soft plunk sounded close ahead. Pan-sook, who had been moving with stamina and sureness, stumbled and fell. Mots-kay leaped to one side to avoid running into his friend—and then he saw the Eutaw, crouched in the low bushes a short distance ahead. The man had a bow in one hand, and the other hand was reaching back over his shoulder for an arrow. His eyes were black with hatred and fear, and surprise too. Mots-kay knew instantly that he was standing face to face with stark and sudden death.

The young Nimapu had been carrying his bow and an arrow clutched together in the grasp of his left hand. Now, knowing that his life depended on his quick action, his right hand leaped to the arrow's notched end and fitted it to the bowstring. The dark man had his arrow, too, and flipped the stone-headed point of it forward. Mots-kay pulled his bowstring with a single, desperate movement; then the shaft was gone from between his thumb and forefinger.

The Eutaw's own bow was half drawn, when his eyes suddenly widened to a fixed stare. His hand loosened on the arrow, which spurted weakly forward to dig its point harmlessly into the ground. The man's knee collapsed and he slumped forward, falling on his face in the dirt.

Mots-kay hastily gazed around in apprehension —but no other Eutaw bows appeared. His eyes came back to the man on the ground. He recognized him as the stumbling runner who had lagged behind the others. Evidently the man had become exhausted and halted to rest; his companions had probably gone on.

Mots-kay wheeled to his rear. "Pan-sook—!" he called in alarm. The young Shoshonee was lying in a strangely awkward position. His legs moved feebly. Mots-kay reached down, caught him by the shoulder, and turned him over. The broken shaft of an arrow protruded from near the center of his chest. "Pan-sook—?" Mots-kay cried again, anxiously. There was no answer; and looking at the dull, clouded eyes, he knew there would never be. The muscles of Mots-kay's throat tightened painfully.

Death and separation were commonplace in that harsh and primitive world, and Mots-kay knew them well. But this had happened with such terrible and shocking swiftness. Mots-kay had a shattering feeling of empty helplessness. He felt more alone than ever before in his life. He and Pan-sook had been together so many months, had undergone so many hardships and dangers and disappointments together! Now Pan-sook was gone. It seemed to Mots-kay that a part of himself was missing, that he had suddenly been made small and unimportant. His throat went dry with the realization that, but for a whim of fate, it might easily be him lying there with an enemy arrow in his chest.

A sudden, powerful impulse came to him to turn directly toward his home in the deep canyon country—to forget all else and travel as swiftly as he could to the safety of his village, avoiding all other dangers until he was there. To get back safely was the important thing; that, he realized now, was what Pan-sook had believed. Somehow the feeling—the knowledge, perhaps—that he would not reach his home had been in Pan-sook's heart. But Mots-kay knew that there had never been any fear there—not even at the very last. And Mots-kay knew, too, that he could not abandon his dream and forget about the beautiful stallion—not now after all that had happened.

Awareness of his surroundings returned to him. The Eutaw lying in the low brush was still, his face down in the dirt, the fingers of one hand lifeless about the bow.

But where were the others? Would they be coming back to look for their fallen comrade? Mots-kay did not think they would; they were too intent on capturing the horses. But he could not be sure. He had the feeling that he should get away from this place as soon as possible. In a second encounter with the Eutaws he could hardly hope to be so fortunate.

But first Pan-sook had to be properly started on his long journey to the Spirit Land. That was of great importance.

The crude arrows had spilled from their bark holder. Mots-kay carefully put them back. He lifted Pan-sook's limp form to his shoulder and bent to pick up the bow. Then he went back through the valley, looking for a place now remembered—a steep bank of dry, crumbly earth. When he came to it he put Pan-sook down at the foot of the bank and, with his hands and a stick, hollowed out a shallow grave. He then placed his dead friend in this, making sure that the food pouch, even though empty, and the good knife of the white man's metal were in their proper places. The bow Mots-kay laid beside Pan-sook, so it would be ready to his left hand when he needed it. The coiled rope, with which he had led the Red One for so many days, was placed at his other side. Who could tell? There might be a horse to keep him company when he reached the Happy Hunting Ground.

Mots-kay climbed to the bank above and jumped on it, caving down the loose, dry dirt. He kept pushing at it with his feet, making small avalanches, until it formed a slanting, unbroken slope that covered the grave deeply and completely. Now that section of the bank, because of the newly exposed moistness, was darker than the rest, but Mots-kay knew that the sun and the dry air would soon erase this difference. Pan-sook could rest there undisturbed until he entered into the next life. Mots-kay could only hope that this new existence would be kinder to the young Shoshonee who had so desperately yearned to return to the land of his people.

Turning his footsteps back up the valley, Mots-kay cautiously approached the place where the dead Eutaw lay. The man was as Mots-kay had last seen him. The youth moved closer, staring curiously and wondering about this Indian who had reacted to their appearance with such swift violence. It was plain that the Eutaws expected no mercy and gave none.

The man's bow was a good one, of dark, well-seasoned wood, strong and finely curved. Mots-kay took it, and also the fringed case that contained the arrows. The Eutaw had been carrying with him five good moccasins, three of them stuffed with dried meat, hung by strings from his shoulders. Mots-kay lifted the strings to his own shoulders thankfully, knowing two of his most pressing problems would thus be eased.

The robe was big, and made of well-dressed skins. Mots-kay pulled it free. Two pouches were tied at the dead man's waist. The small one Mots-kay believed to contain a sacred bundle—a very personal thing between a man and the spirits—and he did not touch it. In the other pouch were a worn stone knife, a bone awl, a hardened fire drill, a small bag of paint,

133

a smoking pipe, and several stone arrow points. The paint was smooth and bright red. Mots-kay tied the long strings of this pouch about his own waist; then he climbed from the valley floor to a high shoulder, from which he could see the land ahead.

He knew this action would cost him time, but now there was a new danger on the trail: the possibility of meeting a Eutaw, or perhaps more than one, returning to look for their missing companion. Mots-kay did not think this likely—but it could happen, and he did not feel that he should risk it.

Holding to the ridge the rest of the day, he scouted the country to the front carefully. Neither horses nor men, nor even any dust, were to be seen, however; and he began to worry whether he was going in the right direction. Near sundown he ventured back down into the valley and was reassured at finding the trail again there—two horses and three men, all traveling at a walk.

A high point loomed ahead. Climbing it, Mots-kay watched the broken countryside round about while darkness came. The fire he had thought he might see did not appear. He ate some of the dried meat from the dead Eutaw's moccasins and lay down on the robe, pleased by its warmth and large size.

In the morning the young Nimapu went on, holding to a course above the winding canyon. Finally, however, it was necessary to descend to the valley again to make certain that the trail was still there below. Mots-kay picked up the trail; but it soon left the valley and ascended a side slope to lead over a rise and downward into another valley. Able to see well ahead, Mots-kay did not vary his steady jog. Farther on, the tracks turned into an offshoot draw, and from here pointed into more uneven country.

The end of the bright, warm day found Mots-kay studying this rough terrain in the last light, giving careful attention to the ravines ahead. He saw nothing to either alarm or encourage him. He went down the slope to a waterhole for the night. Now he felt Pan-sook's absence keenly; and, after eating, he sat for a while in moody thought. Why had he been selected as the one to live? There could be only one reason—to take the spotted stallion back to his people.

The meat from the moccasin was neither pounded nor completely dried. It had evidently been prepared on the trail, which strengthened Mots-kay's belief that these Eutaws were a long way from their village. He considered this a helpful circumstance, because no more of them would be likely to appear.

The last tracks that he had taken time to look at carefully had shown that the men were not very far ahead of him, sometimes walking and at other times trotting. He had to catch up—but also he had to be cautious. Three against one were heavy odds, especially when the three were fierce and cunning Eutaws.

Morning came clear and glaring. Mots-kay got up, gathered his possessions, and started on. The trail was plain in some places and faint in others. Despite his steady traveling, however, it seemed no fresher than on the previous day. But faith in his wyakin and dogged determination kept him going. Toward afternoon he increased his gait to a jog. Then, late in the day, as he crossed a divide between two valleys, he saw something that brought him to a sudden halt. It was a thin blue column of smoke rising in the air from the green trees that bordered the stream below.

Quickly Mots-kay backed into the nearest cover and squatted there, every sense keenly alert. It was a fire—made most probably by the Eutaws. But why in the daytime? Had they finally given up? Were they there, or had they perhaps gone on? And where were the horses? Had the Eutaws caught them? All these questions flooded into his mind, all demanding answers.

Other than the smoke, Mots-kay could see nothing of importance, and no sound reached his straining ears. The smoke was thin and rose lazily, telling of a fire that had not recently had fresh wood. The Eutaws might have cooked and eaten some food, and then gone on. If so, Mots-kay would lose valuable time by waiting. On the other hand, they might still be down there.

He remained there, cautious in his uncertainty. The sun turned red in its decline and the shadows grew long and darker. The blue of the smoke faded against the green—and then it was night.

At last, Mots-kay heard sounds: the faint cracking noises of dead limbs being broken. Soon a rosy glow became visible against the lower branches of the cottonwoods; it steadily increased in size and intensity. One of Mots-kay's questions had been answered. The men were there.

A little later he left the bushes and moved cautiously downward through the darkness. In the bottom, between the tree trunks, he saw the fire—a small but steady flame. The light fell against one dark figure, squatting near a suspended cooking paunch. Where were the others? Mots-kay moved with great caution until he glimpsed them, one lying on a robe and the other sitting with his back against a tree. Beyond the fire the rear half of a deer hung red from a limb.

Presently the men gathered about the paunch and began to dip in for the chunks of boiled meat. They ate until the paunch was empty, then sprawled onto their robes without even taking the precaution of quenching the fire, which provided reassurance to Mots-kay. It was plain that the Eutaws had no suspicion of his presence.

The dark forms soon became completely still.

137

CHAPTER 13

Where were the horses? That was the big question.

Mots-kay made his way around the camp, treading softly. The Eutaws, he believed, would not stir again until dawn; and he intended that, by that time, it would make little difference if they did see his tracks.

At the creek he stooped to drink before crossing over a shallow riffle. Gliding on among the trees, he searched the darkness for a gray form and stopped at regular intervals to listen for the stamp of a hoof or the swish of a tail. The smell of smoke was strong, and the coals of the fire gave a red gleam. The dark shapes of the sleeping men had not changed their attitudes.

If the horses had been caught, they would be tied, Mots-kay reasoned, here among the trees. But they were not to be seen. Mots-kay frowned and shook his head. The unhurried, satisfied manner of the Eutaws was hard to explain, if they had not caught the horses.

Leaving the trees, he crossed to the foot of a short,

steep rise. Here the stargleam was brighter, and he paused before climbing to the bench above. Earlier, from the opposite slope, he had been able to see that area, and no horses were there. But they had to be somewhere and, because they were so tired, Mots-kay was sure they would not have continued far after their pursuers had halted.

He then made a wide circle over the gently sloping bench. Once, he caught sight of a dim gray shape, which moved when he approached it with quickened hope. But the thud of the hoofs identified a bounding deer.

Returning to the lip of the bench, Mots-kay sat down, weary and puzzled. What had happened? Where were the horses? Had the men given up and ceased to follow them? He wished he could believe that—but he did not. These Eutaws were not the kind of men that gave up, not when possession of two highly valued horses was the prize.

Too tired for further random searching, Mots-kay found a hiding place near the rim and crawled into it. At dawn, as the light increased, he carefully surveyed the creek bottom and the slopes around him. A small herd of deer browsed high on the opposite slope, too far away from the Eutaws' camp to be alarmed.

Smoke did not appear above the trees until well after sunup, and Mots-kay knew that the men were not in any hurry. His eyes continued to search the valley below and the country around with dogged persistence. Notched on the far side of the creek was the steep-walled narrow mouth of a short intersecting canyon. Mots-kay had noticed this feature before—but now he saw something else. A short way into the gap, where it was narrowest, there was a solid wall of dead, dry brush and limbs, piled head high.

Mots-kay's eyes narrowed to thin, thoughtful slits. Someone had gone to a lot of trouble to heap the brush and limbs in that place. Why? There could be only one reason: to hold something back!

After a quick look to make sure no one would see him from below, the youth squirmed out of his hiding place, jumped to his feet, and ran along the bench in an upstream direction through the bright morning sunshine. At a point well away from the camp, he made his way down the slope and then leaped from boulder to boulder across the creek. With almost reckless haste he climbed the opposite slope and, at its summit, ran swiftly across the open benchland. Arriving at the edge of the intersecting canyon, he threw himself down on his stomach for a look over the lip of broken rock.

One glance was all he needed. There, in the bottom—so close that he could toss a pebble to them—were the two horses, one spotted white and the other red. And, looking about at the steep walls, Mots-kay could see no way by which they might escape. He knew at once that the horses were finally trapped in this high-walled prison after the relentless chase. The easy, pleased manner of the Eutaws was now explained.

But they had not won—not yet! Mots-kay searched the sheer rock sides for a place where he could drop over the rim and slide down the slope of shattered stone and earth to the canyon floor. A hole could then be quickly opened through the brush barrier. Once outside with the horses, he would find some way to elude the Eutaws. His wyakin, he was certain, would help him.

Mots-kay was just ready to let himself down over the rim when his eye caught a movement near the barrier. He became completely still. It was a man on the brush wall; and while Mots-kay watched, he dropped inside. Immediately two more men appeared and joined the first. Mots-kay knew he was too late, for any movement he made now would be sure to be seen immediately.

The men came along the canyon floor, walking alertly. The one in front carried a lance, and Mots-kay saw that it was the tall leader—who, despite his fierceness, seemed to be in constant fear of sudden attack. All three of them wore only moccasins and breechclouts, and each carried a rope coiled in his hands.

The stallion swung his head about, looking at the dark, sheer walls; then he gave ground, backing reluctantly. The mare turned and trotted back along the canyon floor. When the stallion followed her, Mots-kay saw that he limped painfully on his right front foot. Too, both horses were so thin that their ribs showed plainly through their bright summer coats. They had their heads up, suspiciously watching everything behind them. Long days of running had taught them what to expect from these grim pursuers.

Then the animals halted and turned to face the Indians. The stallion was nervous but defiant, reminding Mots-kay of the way he had acted when the Spaniards carried sticks and shovels into his pen. He would fight, Mots-kay knew, but how could that help? The men came on, grimly determined. Mots-kay could see their glossy black hair and their lean, coppery shoulders glinting in the sun. He hated them for what they were doing to the Spotted One—for the unfeeling, merciless way in which they had driven the horse to lameness and exhaustion.

The mare moved on along the wall and the stallion trailed after her, turning his upflung head from side to side to watch behind. Despite his weariness and his sore feet, Mots-kay saw, his spirit was still staunch and proud.

At its upper end the canyon squeezed to a small nook—the last retreat. The mare came to this and paused, evidently realizing that there was no way out. When the men pressed closer, she entered. The stallion followed, crowding against her, increasing her nervous fear by his own anxiety.

The three men paused. The tall leader in front raised his lance in a threatening gesture that caused the mare to turn and breast the rubble slope. Placing her feet carefully she slowly picked her way upward. Loose earth slid behind her in small avalanches about the ankles of the stallion, who was following. At the foot of the sheer wall she stopped, unable to go any farther. The stallion crowded up against her and turned crosswise, his hard, dark hoofs seeking solid footing in the yielding earth.

The men trudged upward awkwardly through the sliding dirt, ropes ready in their hands. The leader's lance waved in his hand as he used his long arms to maintain his balance. The stallion wheeled in fright hard against the mare and turned back on jittery legs. Loose earth and rock gave way under his feet. Suddenly he plunged downward, half falling but managing to keep upright. Then Mots-kay saw his ears flatten against his dark neck as the powerful jaws flew open.

The Eutaw in the horse's path yelled wildly and sought to dodge aside, but his feet also slipped. Horse and man went down together, in a rolling, tangled mass, to the foot of the slope. There the stallion found his footing and staggered up; but the man did not move.

The leader and the other man bounded down the

slant, screeching angrily. The Spotted One reared in the roiling dust. Mots-kay caught a glimpse of his powerful front legs slashing at the air. The tall leader recoiled, then savagely hurled his lance. The next instant he was caught under the merciless pounding of the hard hoofs and disappeared down into the blinding dust.

The third man broke and ran desperately back along the canyon floor. Out of the dust behind came the stallion, galloping wildly, screaming in pain and rage. He overtook the man in the narrow gap and knocked him sprawling, then raced on.

The Eutaw rolled and lay still a moment, then pushed himself up dazedly. Wheeling to a halt, the stallion let out a snorting blast. The man turned to the slope across the canyon from Mots-kay and started climbing frantically. He fell once, but regained himself and clawed his way upward again. Reaching the sheer rock wall, he found a crevice leading up to the rim and disappeared into it.

Mots-kay knew that this was his opportunity. Swinging his legs over the ledge, he dropped to the slope and went down it in long, plunging strides. A glance to the upper end of the canyon showed him that both of the Eutaws were lying motionless where they had fallen.

The stallion snorted again, still in a state of wild excitement. Mots-kay forced himself to slow to a walk and said gently, "Do not be afraid, Spotted One. It is Mots-kay, who brought the good grass to you in the pen."

The horse's eyes were wide and distrustful. At the sound of the youth's voice his ears swiveled backward, then forward again. He was bleeding badly from a wound in his chest. "Do not be afraid," repeated Mots-kay. "I shall not hurt you. I shall take you away from these bad men who are trying to catch you."

The stallion stood there uncertainly, but he moved away nervously when the Indian tried to approach. "Stay. There is not much time," Mots-kay pleaded in a low voice. He shot another glance toward the upper end of the canyon but could see nothing moving there. "Stay, Spotted One."

The stallion was still trembling from fright and excitement, though he seemed unaware of the blood trickling down his foreleg. He turned and retreated a few steps, then paused to look back over his shoulder.

"Wait. Let me catch you."

The stallion turned slowly to face him. Mots-kay approached, keeping his rope behind him and holding out his cupped hand as if something was in it. The horse jerked his nose up warily. The youth halted, hoping desperately that no more Eutaws would appear. He made himself speak gently. "Be still, Spotted One. It is Mots-kay, who fed you and rubbed your back and shoulders with the brush to clean your hair."

Finally, after what seemed a desperately long time, the stallion let him approach and sniffed his outstretched hand. "Be still, Spotted One. There is not much time." The Indian's hand rubbed the dusty mottled muzzle and scratched the deep recess between the heavy jowls—an attention that Mots-kay knew the stallion keenly enjoyed. When he saw that the horse was reassured, he slipped his rope about the dark neck and firmly tied a strong knot.

He shot another quick glance up the canyon and said urgently, "Come! We must go at once." The stallion followed without any hesitation.

Mots-kay tore an opening through one end of the brush barrier large enough to let the horse pass through. As he worked, an unexpected noise from behind suddenly caused him to whirl fearfully—but it was only the red mare, following along after the stallion as she usually did. Mots-kay had almost forgotten her; and now he frowned, not at all certain that he wanted her to come. Pan-sook was no longer there, and anyway it would be difficult enough to escape with one horse alone. But he did not have the heart to turn her back.

"All right, come on—if you must," Mots-kay told her, and turned to take the stallion's lead rope. "But

146

you had better keep up, and not cause any trouble," he added in stern warning. The mare followed with a doglike faithfulness.

When they had cleared the canyon mouth, Mots-kay set off in the upstream direction, away from the Eutaw camp. He could only guess what would happen back there, but he knew that he should put as much distance as possible between himself and those bitterly frustrated men.

The horses at first accepted a brisk pace without reluctance. But after they had been traveling a while the stallion began to limp more heavily. Presently he pulled back to a halting walk. Mots-kay knew he had to go more slowly, regardless of the danger that might be behind. He shortened his stride, giving the stallion more time, and kept a sharp watch to the rear.

The sun had moved well past its midday point. Mots-kay let the two horses stop to graze, and they lowered their heads hungrily. As the youth listened to their busy jaws he scanned the back trail. Where were the Eutaws? Their leader might have been badly hurt, even killed—and the other two would be bruised and sore. They might not be so eager to start again.

But he did not dare to wait any longer. "Come on," he said, and gave the stallion's rope a tug. The red mare lifted her head and followed as obediently as if there were a rope on her neck, too. "You can stay and eat," Mots-kay told her gruffly, knowing very well that she would not.

Late in the afternoon the stallion's limp became still worse. It was plain that he had to rest. Mots-kay halted, looked around, and then dropped the rope. He set off along the back trail, certain that the tired horse would be there when he returned. Mounting a shoulder of land, he watched the countryside they had crossed until long after dark. Though he saw nothing of the Eutaws, still he did not relax his vigilance. Near midnight he made his way back to the horses. They were quiet in the darkness, hardly moving as he approached. He patted the stallion on the neck, then lay down on the grass and went to sleep.

They were moving again before daylight, but all through the long, hot day their progress was distressingly slow. Survey of the back country revealed no signs of pursuit. Perhaps the men were not following, Mots-kay thought.

He kept on until midafternoon. Then the stallion halted and stood with his big head low. Mots-kay pulled gently a couple of times, then dropped the rope. Something, he realized, was wrong—something beyond just weariness. Mots-kay moved around to examine the wound in the horse's chest, and the frown on his young face deepened. Not much raw flesh was exposed; but what Mots-kay could see had a dark, unhealthy look.

He had seen such a look before, and at once he became deeply anxious. "No," he said to himself bitterly. "It must not happen. The wound must heal. It is the desire of my wyakin, revealed to me in a vision."

Then, in the little glade, the Nimapu stood beside the feeble horse and prayed to the Indian gods for a long time, his youthful face raised to the heavens. The Spotted One must not die now. Not after all he had been through—the long journeys, the harsh months of slavery, Pan-sook's sudden death.

In the evening the red mare began to graze, and the stallion stirred as if he would accompany her. Then a stiffness in his legs could be seen, and when he put his head down it was plain that he could open his heavy jaws only with great difficulty. After trying to eat for a short while, he gave up the effort and became still.

Mots-kay knew that the evil in the wound was hard at work. He went to the horse and sang for him. He sang in a low, pleading voice—sang all the healing songs that he knew, asking the spirits to use their miraculous powers in behalf of the sick animal.

The night passed slowly. Mots-kay kindled a small fire and sat cross-legged before it. The stallion finally folded his stiff joints and lay down, dropping to the earth heavily. Some time later he sighed deeply, rolled on his side, and let his big, proud head come to rest on the cold earth.

Mots-kay sat beside the horse, listening and hoping and praying for the moment when the labored breathing would become easier—when the heat of the fever would burn itself out. But the moment did not come. Just as the sky was beginning to glow with the coming of a new morning, the stallion gave a last, desperate gasp; then his breathing ceased entirely.

CHAPTER 14

Mots-kay could not believe it. The beautiful spotted stallion—the horse revealed to him by his wyakin—could not be dead!

But not the slightest flicker of life remained under his hand.

The grief in Mots-kay's heart became slowly smothering, so that he could hardly breathe. All of his hopes and plans had been crushed, leaving him nothing. Why had this terrible thing happened to him? Had he in some manner proved unworthy? It must be so. His fine horse would never again whinny a welcome when he came with grass, or nudge his shoulder in appreciation. Nor would he proudly be leading a spotted stallion when he returned to his village.

Day—fresh, clean, and golden—spread across the land. The mare stirred from her resting place and began to graze. Mots-kay suddenly resented her. Why, he thought, do you live! You have no spots, no

151

beauty. You do not even sorrow that the Spotted One is dead. But then he saw that he could not be sure of that, for the mare's big eyes were dark and solemn. Noticing her gaunt flanks, Mots-kay forgave her in his heart for eating at this time.

He fumbled in one of the moccasins he had taken from the dead Eutaw, found a piece of dried meat, and chewed it slowly. Where were the hated Eutaws? The tall leader who had thrown his lance into the Spotted One's chest did not deserve to live. He hoped the others were hurt, too.

But what now for him? What was left? He felt he was an outcast, forsaken by the spirits he had believed in.

The sun made its morning climb into the sky, rapidly at first and then more slowly. Mots-kay did not move. His thoughts, dark and moody, turned to his dead friend Pan-sook. The young Shoshonee had been the wise one—he had known it would all be useless. And perhaps he was the more fortunate, too: he would never know such pain and despair.

Finally Mots-kay got to his feet. The sun was bright and the earth was warm and fragrant. But the spotted stallion was dead. The Nimapu tribe would never see the unbelievable beauty of that coat. If he told his people of a horse so beautifully colored, they would never believe it!

Then a new thought came to his mind. He considered it for several long seconds before coming to a decision. Yes, he could make them believe it. He would do it.

Taking out the good Spanish knife, Mots-kay tested the edge. It was sharp—but not sharp enough for what he had in mind. With a small stone from his pouch he carefully whetted the blade. Presently, satisfied, he went to the dead stallion. He gazed downward a long moment, and then bent to the task.

Skinning animals and dressing hides might be "women's work"; but, while a slave among the Eutaws, Mots-kay had become highly skilled at it. Now he was thankful for the drudgery and the training. For this must be a perfect skin—one so natural that no one could question the striking beauty of the horse it had once covered. Every stroke of the strong blade was made with thoughtful care and skill.

It took a long time; but at last the hide was free in Mots-kay's hands. He spread it on the grass, the side covered with the gleaming hair facing upward. Then he folded it into a compact bundle. Using strong strips cut from his robe, he tied the bundle, making two loops for his shoulders. Wet and fresh, the hide was heavy; but Mots-kay knew he could carry it back to his village. He was determined that his people should see it.

Then Mots-kay noticed the red mare watching him

curiously with her big, dark eyes. Another thought took shape. Why not? She was not the fine stallion of his dreams—but she was a horse, and therefore useful in carrying burdens. He went to her and knotted the rope about her neck.

For her back, the bundle needed to be of a different shape—long and supple enough to bend in the middle. He spread out the hide once again on the grass and refolded it. The mare's eyes widened suspiciously when he carried it to her. "Be still, Red One," he commanded. "It is the Spotted One's hide. I wish to take it to my village to show to my people. It will not hurt you."

She stood quietly, and Mots-kay balanced the bundle over the sharp ridge of her back. The limp folds hung down on either side, and he fastened the straps under her belly and around her chest to tie the skin in place. "Come," he said when he had finished, and took up the rope.

The mare's hoofs were deeply worn and her ribs plainly visible, but she followed with cheerful obedience. They traveled steadily, and Mots-kay soon came to appreciate her gentle willingness. Late in the afternoon he took the pack from her back to let her graze. He unfolded the skin and stretched it on clean grass, using small pegs in holes punched at the edges. With twists of grass as sponges, he washed away the bloodstains. Then he left the hide spread out to air and dry during the night.

One day followed another. No Eutaws appeared, and as time went on, Mots-kay became increasingly hopeful that they would not. But when he came to a high point of land he would still turn for long looks at the country behind. Because of his own weariness and the mare's worn feet, he found he had to shorten his march each day. Each day he worked on the horsehide, scraping and cleaning. Also he had to stop and hunt when he ran out of food.

The days became shorter and the nights colder. Remembering the high mountains ahead, Mots-kay forced himself to increase his travel time. But when the mountains were in sight, their crests were already white with snow. The youth hurried on, hoping he could get through. The weather turned dark and stormy, and rain slowed his progress. When the clouds cleared, the snowline had moved well down the slopes.

It was the first snow that Mots-kay had seen in many months; but he knew from long experience in his native mountains that the high passes would soon be closed, if they were not already. He pushed on, now more anxious than ever to get home. The snow in the canyons deepened. He climbed and kept to the windblown ridges, his robe wrapped close against the cold.

The mare's hair was now long and thick, and her ribs no longer showed. But one afternoon, struggling through the knee-deep drifts, Mots-kay realized that she would never make it over the summit. She had proved herself to be strong and willing, and she would try . . . but she couldn't get through. No horse could.

Looking up at the smooth, white slopes, he thought for a long time. He had a good bow and a warm robe. On snowshoes, traveling alone, he could do it; and he could himself carry the spotted hide, which, now thoroughly dried, was much lighter. He turned and looked at the mare, knowing he would have to leave her. Doubtless she would be glad to get back to the lower country, where it was not so cold and there was grass to eat.

A clump of small, young trees stuck up through the snow a short distance away. Mots-kay cut two long, slender lengths of the tough green wood, bent them into rough circles, and lashed the ends together with stout lengths of rawhide. But before he had completed the webbing in even one of the frames, the supply of leather in his pouch was exhausted. Wondering what else he might use, he thought of the pouch itself, the extra moccasins, and the long bow case—all of which could be cut into strips. Finally, however, he cut the needed pieces from the edge of his robe, though he knew the warmth thus sacrificed would be sorely missed during the cold nights to come.

The crude snowshoes finished, Mots-kay went to the red mare, untied the bundle from her back, and shifted it to his own. Grabbing her mane, he turned her about so that she was headed back along the deep, ragged trail they had made in the snow in coming up the slope. "Go on. Go back," he said to her. "There is grass for you down in the valleys."

She took a step or two, then halted and looked back, as if puzzled because he was not coming.

Mots-kay turned away, with no time to waste. He quickly lashed the snowshoes to his feet and started trudging upward through the soft whiteness.

Even with the snowshoes the traveling was not easy—and the snow above would be still deeper and more difficult. But Mots-kay was determined to get through the pass. He had come too far and had been through too much to stop now.

On he went, lifting the snowshoes high and crushing the snow down beneath them. But his steps were short, and the progress was slow.

Presently the young Indian had to pause to catch his breath. Turning slightly, he let his glance go back down the slope—and his eyes widened with surprise and wonder. The red mare, lifting her forelegs in high, weary lunges, was fighting her way up through the snow to follow him.

"Go back!" he called angrily. "Go back! You cannot get through the pass. There is no food for you. You will die up here!"

The mare stopped her lunging and stood looking at him, the snow above her knees.

"Go back!" Mots-kay cried again; but after a minute's rest she began once more, gamely fighting her way upward toward him.

"No, no," the young Nimapu muttered bitterly. He became silent, not knowing what to do.

This seemed to encourage the mare, and she came on, not halting until she was only a few feet below him.

"What is the matter with you?" Mots-kay blurted at her. But despite his anger, he knew then that he would not leave her. She was too loyal and obedient, too patient and understanding. She had been a part of his life, and of Pan-sook's, ever since the night they had dug their way through the high Spanish wall. He turned about on the clumsy snowshoes so that he could push his way back along the trail downhill.

"Come on, follow me, Red One," he told the horse gently. "We shall find a good place to spend the winter in some valley below, and come back in the spring, when the snow turns to water and the high meadows will be green with sweet grass."

CHAPTER 15

At the top of a wide, grassy slope Mots-kay halted. His face brightened joyously. "The white smoke yonder is from the cooking pits," he told the red mare. "The mush of the camass root will be hot and tender and sweet. It is the village of my people."

Then he realized that he was trembling—trembling with excitement and a strange uneasiness. It had been so long, so many moons ago. He had left his people when he had been only a boy, unknowing and foolishly boastful. Now, after all the long months, he was returning, without the horse that he had promised he would bring. Mots-kay felt as if he were a stranger. How would they receive him?

Still, he was not coming empty handed. He *was* bringing a horse—the wonderfully gentle and intelligent red mare—and a beautiful spotted robe. And he had proved himself in killing an enemy. He lifted his head and pushed back his shoulders. His return should be in fitting style, so as to be well remembered.

Mots-kay thought of the little bag of paint he had taken from the dead Eutaw. He got it out of his pouch and, using a finger as a brush, streaked his sun-blackened face with red lines, drawing them backward and upward from his mouth and chin. He put other lines on his chest and upper arms, pleased by the bright color.

His eyes came to rest on the mare. She looked drab. If only he had some long feathers, he could tie them to her mane and tail. He tried the paint—but it did not show well against her already red coat. Now, if it were the silvery coat of the beautiful spotted stallion. . . .

A thought came to Mots-kay—a sudden, daring thought. That *would* be something that they would not soon forget!

He untied the straps from the Red One and spread the robe on the grass. The sunlight caught its whiteness and vivid spotting—and once more he felt a quick pang of disappointment in his heart. But he forced himself to ignore the pain.

My wyakin has said that I shall bring a spotted horse, he thought, and I shall. My people will see it.

Gathering up the robe, he spread it on the mare's back. She stood quietly as he smoothed it over her strong withers and back along her loins, covering

161

her red coat with one of gleaming silver white. Then, making small holes in the robe, he tied it in place with strips of deerhide and stepped back for a longer look.

Suddenly Mots-kay had a fleeting feeling that the spotted stallion had come to life again. In his eyes the revelation of his wyakin had been fulfilled in a beautiful and striking way.

The young Indian stood there, straight and tall. "Now," he declared, "Mots-kay will return to his people. Come, Spotted One."

Two lean, coppery boys, stalking a long-eared rabbit in a clump of brush, stared briefly with wide, wondering eyes. Then they fled toward the huts of their village, screeching at the tops of their voices.

At this wild alarm everyone within hearing pulled to quick attention. Men ran from the huts and lodges clutching their bows and arrows, thrusting kopluts, or war clubs, into their belts. Women and girls hurried along the paths from the camass sloughs, still grasping their horn-handled digging sticks.

Mots-kay advanced at a dignified pace, looking to neither right nor left.

The men quickly formed a close group of dark, half-naked bodies and moved forward, arrows set challengingly against their bowstrings. Then they halted, silently awaiting the stranger's approach.

Mots-kay strode on until he was standing before

162

them. Theirs were the faces of men who did not know him. But he recognized old Eagle-on-a-Rock, the village chief, and Wounded Elk, and No Toes— his own father.

"Who is it that comes with a mistatim, wearing a robe so impossibly colored?" Eagle-on-a-Rock demanded.

It had been many long months since Mots-kay had heard his own language, and he had almost forgotten the word *mistatim,* meaning "big dog," which the Nimapu Indians used to signify a horse. "It is not an impossible color," he replied quickly. "There was a horse of this color. This is his skin."

"That is difficult to believe," retorted Eagle-on-a-Rock. "No one here has ever seen such a horse. Where did you find it?"

"In the village of the men with hair on their faces."

"Men with hair on their faces . . . ?"

"Yes. Their village is a long journey to the south, where there is never any ice or snow. They have many horses."

Eagle-on-a-Rock's eyes narrowed under his shaggy gray brows. He demanded, "Why are you here? What has brought you to the land of the Nimapu?"

"Do my people not know me? I am Mots-kay, the son of No Toes."

"Mots-kay . . . ?" Eagle-on-a-Rock repeated uncertainly.

But No Toes limped forward eagerly and gripped both of Mots-kay's arms with his hands. "My son, it is truly you," he said. "I had all but given up hope that you were still alive." He paused, choked with his great happiness.

Before Mots-kay could reply, cries of recognition came from some of the others.

"It is Mots-kay! I know him now!"

"He has grown!"

"He is a man!"

One of them turned and shouted loudly for the village to hear. "It is Mots-kay, the son of No Toes! It is Mots-kay, who went on the long journey to the country of the Shoshonees! Now he returns. It is Mots-kay, the son of No Toes . . . !"

This brought a general rush of boys, women, and girls from the huts. They came and gathered around, their eyes wide and excited. Among them Mots-kay saw Woman-Stands-Tall, his mother. She did not speak nor crowd in with the others—but Mots-kay saw that her eyes were gleaming with joy.

The people swarmed about Mots-kay and his horse. True to her gentle nature, the red mare stood patiently, even when jostled by the pushing crowd. Mots-kay was proud of her.

A man pushed forward to confront Mots-kay. It was Wounded Elk, who had led the Nimapu party to the Shoshonee country. "What happened?" he asked. "Were you ambushed?"

"Yes. The young Shoshonee and I were taken by the Eutaws as slaves. But he is dead now. He was a brave man—but he did not live to return to his village."

"A council!" someone cried. "Let us have a council, so all can hear of these happenings on the great journey from which Mots-kay is returning. He has much to tell."

"Prepare the council place; make the fire," ordered the chief. "Mots-kay will tell us of the long journey to the country of the strange people. And he will tell us of the horse that was both light and dark, and had the spots on its back."

The people hastened to a well-worn area near the center of the encampment. Women brought dry twigs and limbs, and a small fire was kindled. The chief and the respected elders took their accustomed places of honor; a ceremonial pipe was brought and lighted. Mots-kay led his horse to the place reserved for them and waited silently while the chief and the elders puffed the pipe to each of the four corners of the earth.

The men of the tribe had seated themselves in a big circle, surrounding the elders, the fire, and the young man with his horse. Just outside this circle the older boys, the women, and the girls were gathered, their dark, wide-boned faces alive with interest.

When the smoking rites were finished and the people were quiet, Eagle-on-a-Rock said in his full,

strong voice, "Tell us of the journey which has kept you from our village for so many moons, Mots-kay. Tell us of the strange people who have hair on their faces, and of the things that happened in the faraway country that is always warm. And tell us of the horse with the unbelievable colors."

Mots-kay stood by the fire, his tall, dark form erect and lean to the bone from the lengthy traveling. The happiness of being home, among his own people once more, showed in his eyes.

He began his tale. He told them how he and Pan-sook had been taken prisoner by Eutaws leaping from behind boulders. He told them of the many long moons passed as slaves in the Eutaw village—carrying wood and water, scraping hides, doing the work of women. He told them of being taken by their Eutaw masters on a horse-seeking journey to the Spanish settlement, and there being traded by the greedy Eutaws for horses. He told them of the Span-iards and their great magic, and of how the white men were carried in saddles on their horses' backs.

Eagle-on-a-Rock's dark old face wrinkled in a deep, perplexed frown. "Why was that?" he asked. "Can they not walk?"

"Yes, they can walk," Mots-kay answered, "but they do not like to. They like their horses to carry them. It is not so tiring, and they can go very fast— faster than a man can run."

Eagle-on-a-Rock and some of the others shook their heads. "How is it that they do not fall?" one asked.

"They have saddles," Mots-kay told them.

"Saddles . . . ?" old Eagle-on-a-Rock repeated. "What are those?"

167

Mots-kay shrugged, knowing that it was too much to explain in a few words.

Eagle-on-a-Rock shook his head impatiently. "Tell us more of your journey. That is what we want to hear." Though the wrinkles in his face were deep, his eyes were quick and bright.

Mots-kay went on, telling the people of the spotted stallion—of how he had found the proud animal in the small pen and had carried grass to him from the fields.

"Of all the horses the Spaniards had, the Spotted One was the finest and the most beautiful," he declared. "He was a father horse, and the bearded men valued him because of the spotted young he produced. He was strong and bold; he would fight when he was mistreated. But he liked me and would let me come into his pen. When I first saw him, I knew he was the horse of my vision—the horse my wyakin had revealed. . . ." Here Mots-kay had to pause before going on.

By the time he neared the end of his story, the sun was low and the shadows were creeping across the land of the high prairie. The people sat still and silent, marveling at all that he had related.

"I thought I would bring to my people the fine spotted stallion, the horse of my vision," Mots-kay said, slowly and sadly. "But, as you have heard, it could not be done. This is the Red One—taken from the bearded ones by my friend Pan-sook. When he was killed, she became mine. Now I know she is a fine horse. She wears the skin of the Spotted One, so that all may know I speak the truth when I tell of such a horse."

They could hear the great disappointment in the youth's voice as he finished his tale—the regret that he had not done as well as he should have. He felt that somewhere, somehow, he had failed.

Old Eagle-on-a-Rock was the first to speak. "You have been brave and resourceful, my son," he said earnestly. "You have lived through a great journey and many dangers. You have proved that you are worthy of sitting among the men at the council fires. And you have brought to the Nimapu people not one horse, but two. Her belly is big with something that is not grass."

Mots-kay's forehead furrowed. What did Eagle-on-a-Rock mean? He turned and looked at the Red One—and saw that which had been happening so gradually that he had not realized it before. The mare was big, with the bigness of new life, like the female deer in the spring before the fawns were born. The spotted robe fell short of covering her bulging sides.

Mots-kay remembered the frisky, playful colts at the Spanish settlement. His face brightened with understanding. With great joy and thankfulness in his voice, he said, "I have been blind—but now my eyes are open. My wyakin is very wise and has much power. It is the Red One that will fulfill the vision. The young one that is to come will be a magnificent father horse when it is grown. It will have the coat of the beautiful color, too; for the great Spotted One is most certainly its father. All of you will see this. The Nimapu horses will be many and good. They will serve our people well during the years to come."

Thus it may have been that long ago the Nimapu Indians—later known as the Nez Percés—received their first horse of two colors. The tribe was to become widely admired for the excellence of its herds of spotted ponies. Distinctively marked descendants are known today as Appalousas.

ABOUT THE AUTHOR

Glenn Balch, well-known author of horse and western adventure stories, is a native-born Texan. His first and most cherished possession was a horse; and his early dreams were to be a cowboy or a forest ranger. After he was graduated from Baylor University, his love for the open spaces led him farther westward to Idaho.

Mr. Balch's first job there was in the Forest Service, followed by a stint as a reporter for the *Boise Statesman*. Five years later he came to New York and studied at Columbia University; and while he was in New York his first book was published. He then returned to Idaho, where he now makes his home.

Mr. Balch's horse stories are filled with the information and understanding that he has gained in actual experience in the wild-horse country. His stories of animals and Western adventure have made him a favorite author of young readers throughout the world.

ABOUT THE ILLUSTRATOR

When Lorence Bjorklund was a child in St. Paul, Minnesota, he loved to sit on a bluff overlooking the Mississippi River. Here, close to the burial mounds of Indian chiefs, he daydreamed about the pioneers and Indians who were to figure so prominently in his work as an artist.

From the days when he drew on rolls of surplus wallpaper, Lorence Bjorklund has been primarily interested in illustration. As a young man, he was an apprentice mural painter and later won an art scholarship to Pratt Institute in New York City. He has illustrated well over three hundred books, most of them based on Old West themes. His hobbies are closely associated with his work, for he collects guns, builds scale models of ships and wagons, and studies Indian life at remote camps in the United States and Canada.

Mr. Bjorklund and his family live in Croton Falls, New York, and spend their summers in Maine.